Testimonial

"...The writing grabbed me by the throat and pulled me unresisting into the narrative. I was hooked from the first words, and by the end of the third chapter when yet another shocking element entered the narrative, I was panting for more..."

~ Faye Bolwell

The Accidental Gambler

The Accidental Gambler

A Novel

Cally Berryman (PhD)

Published in Australia by Marble Media
Email: callyberryman@hotmail.com
Website: callyberryman.com
First published in Australia 2018
Copyright © Cally Berryman 2018

Cally Berryman
The Accidental Gambler
ISBN: 9780646954547

Cover photography by Nellie

Cover layout and design by graphic designer

Disclaimer
All care has been taken in the preparation of the information herein, but no responsibility can be accepted by the publisher or author for any damages resulting from the misinterpretation of this work. All contact details given in this book were current at the time of publication but are subject to change.

The advice given in this book is based on the experience of the individuals. Professionals should be consulted for individual problems. The author and publisher shall not be responsible for any person with regard to any loss or damage caused directly or indirectly by the information in this book.

About the author

CALLY BERRYMAN (PHD) WAS BORN IN LESVOS, Greece. She migrated to Australia with her mother and father and two older brothers, John and Jim, in 1952. She is currently employed as a nurse and drug and alcohol and gambling counsellor. She has been employed in nursing and community areas of Drug and Alcohol for over thirty years as a Registered nurse, counsellor, academic, and program development.

Cally's PhD is titled Nurses Drug and Alcohol Use and Dependence: Creating Understanding (University Melbourne).

She has written two books – *The Accidental Gambler* (Fiction) and *Calel (Memoir of a Greek Mother)*. Cally is currently writing a third book

This book is dedicated to the men and women and their families who have been caught in the trap of substance abuse and gambling dependence.

Acknowledgments

My thanks to the following people for their assistance in this novel, either by giving advice or reading sections and providing feedback: Julie Postance, Faye Bolwell, Ann Paterson, Wendy Suvoltos, Jenny O'Sullivan, Peggy Cochrane, Lee Koffman, Sydney Smith.

My thanks to my husband Alan and my family for their support.

Contents

PART 2

PART 3

The End

Introduction
The Accidental Gambler

THE PROTAGONIST, PAULA WILSON, IS A SOCIAL WORKER who is currently employed as an academic at the University of Melbourne. Paula resides in a townhouse in Kensington with her husband, Colin Wilson, and their two daughters, Sarah and Rachael. Colin manages an engineering business from home and is extremely money oriented. At the start of the story, we meet the family celebrating Rachael's birthday, then later the family in turmoil; Rachael is hit by a car and sustains severe head injuries and a leg fracture. The accident impinges on each Wilson family member in different ways; each member develops different coping styles to deal with the tragedy.

The central theme of the novel is the struggle of people to live an authentic, meaningful life despite trauma and setbacks.

PART 1

ONE

Rachael's birthday party
July 2001, Kensington

"OH MY GOD, LOOK AT THE STARS," SAID MADONNA. She pointed to the large gold stars stuck on the driveway.

"Cool, real cool," said Blondie and Tori Amos in unison.

The three girls sprinted to the front entrance and banged on the door.

Loud rock music seeped through the door.

Colin opened the entrance. He wore the clothes of a security man. Long-sleeved black shirt, dark trousers, leather gloves, and dark sunglasses.

"Good evening ladies," he said and made a low bow.

"But first I need to check your invitations," he made a show of pushing his glasses up and peering at each CD-shaped invitation. "Rock party. Let's rock for Rachael's birthday. Dress up as your favourite rock star."

He said, "Mmm" as he checked the names alongside the list.

"Seems all right," he said and stamped each girl's

wrist with a blue star and pinned 'Very Important Person' passes on each girl. "Come this way," he said.

The floor squeaked as they walked; crimson crepe paper made a distinguished entrance.

"I love a red carpet entry," said Blondie, and giggled.

The security man escorted them into the lounge room. Earlier, Paula had emptied the room of furniture and covered the windows with black crepe paper. It resembled a nightclub.

"More rock stars," said Colin, his voice booming over the music. He brandished a torch and shined it over the group of girls dancing in the centre.

"You made it," said Rachael and embraced the newcomers. "Look at you, Madonna!" said Rachael.

The thumping rock music throbbed, lights flickered in the semidarkness. A large multifaceted glass disco ball swayed on the ceiling. Strobe lights flashed red, yellow, and green. Twirls of electric blue and hot pink streamers jumped in time to the music. Windows shook, crockery rattled. The girls danced, hands overextended above heads. Flickering yellow and green lights radiated from glow-stick bracelets. A collection of gold and silver balloons in the corner shook.

Young hips wiggled in time to the music. The dancers grasped ice-cream-cone shaped microphones and sang raucously.

Rachael warbled the loudest, pigtails flying.

Wall posters of Madonna, Blondie, Bjork, and The Rolling Stones watched from the sidelines.

Colin sang; his deep voice rose above the noise.

Silver foil dazzled from the table set on one side of the room. Large plates of nachos, potato crisps, pizzas, and star-shaped sandwiches spread on the table. In the centre of the room, taking pride of place was a large guitar-fashioned cake with 'Rachael' in large lettering.

A camera flashed; then another.

Sister Sarah was the paparazzo on duty.

"Hold that pose," said Sarah as she circled the gyrating dancers.

The girls fashioned extravagant model poses; hands on their hips and pouty faces.

Paula was the designated reporter; she made copious notes on a yellow notepad and moved amongst the dancers.

"Miss Madonna, is it true you came to Australia to buy a house in Essendon?" Paula asked one girl.

"Oh yes, a large one near the river," said the girl.

Jenny, Paula's best friend, wore a black disc jockey's hat and was in charge of the music.

"I have a request for a Blondie number," she said.

At midnight, the strobe lights and music ceased. The rock stars clutched bags of sugared goodies and Polaroid photos. Bemused parents propelled them to waiting cars.

"Group hug," said Rachael, opening her arms wide toward Paula, Colin, Sarah, and Jenny.

A clutch of bodies embraced.

"Thank you, everyone, I've had the best party ever."

"There'll be another party next year," said Jenny, kissing Rachael.

"Not if I go deaf," said Colin.

"My little sister is now ten years old," said Sarah.

TWO

The yellow ribbon
November 2001, Parkville

PAULA WILSON SLUMPS DEEP IN THE GREEN PLASTIC chair as if trying to disappear. She clutches a clump of soggy tissues. Ugly red blotches spread over her face and neck. She runs shaky fingers through uncombed hair. She fidgets in the hard, plastic chair.

Paula is middle-aged, angular. She holds herself like a sprinter—edgy, ready to leap up and race away. Run far from this place of torment. She laces thin fingers over her abdomen as if to ease a cramp, and rocks back and forth.

I hate this place; it gives me the creeps.

She stifles a yawn, gets up, and wanders around the cramped space of cubicle. She circles the bed and crouches under the cables. Finally returns to her chair.

I feel as though I am time travelling; one part of me here and another far away in past terrors.

Again, she feels like a terrified six-year-old, banging against a partition of wood, calling to be let out. She bites on a bent finger, leaving a red mark. Fragments of childish remembrances creep in, intrusive, terrifying. She remembers Sunday school songs.

Jesus loves me this I know, for the Bible tells me so...

The words have no magic anymore. Once she used to kneel on the floor, clasped hands, praying to an unseen higher power. These days, Paula does not kneel, directs soundless applications to whoever is out there.

Please don't let Rachel die.

"Sarah, how are you doing?" she asks the teenager next to her. She squeezes her hand.

"It is all unreal," isn't it?"

"It is so cold in here," said Sarah, shivering.

The collar of her blue-checked school uniform sticks halfway out from the cardigan. She holds the mobile phone and scans her mother's face for clues on how to behave. She turns and squints at Rachael lying still on the hospital bed.

She wants to ask if Rachael will live but is afraid to say the words.

"Paula...," said Colin, the husband.

The words strangle mid-sentence. He feels the room is closing in on him as though the walls are toppling on top of him. He tugs at a dark eyebrow, a habit from childhood. He exhales; it comes out as a groan.

He gets up, bangs the wall of the intensive care cubicle with his fist.

"It's not fair," he said, his voice loud.

The redheaded nurse jolts up from her desk in the cubicle. She goes to Colin and rests a hand on Colin's shoulder.

"Mr Wilson, try to stay calm. Rachael may be unconscious, but she can hear you."

Colin covers his face and sobs.

Paula goes to him, cradles him to her chest. She stretches out an open arm to Sarah. The three grasp each other. When Colin stops crying, she returns to her seat.

She searches for signs of a response from Rachael, tucked under the stark white sheet, notices a smudge of dried blood on Rachael's cheek.

Where is the yellow ribbon from Rachael's pigtail?

This morning Rachael jiggled when Paula threaded the yellow ribbon through the elastic on the pigtail.

"Keep still," Paula had said.

Rachael is unmoving now.

The three are soldiers in a foxhole; it feels like a military zone here.

The family waits for the next grenade attack.

An assortment of intravenous tubes drip into Rachael's body, tiny blue lights move on monitors, machines beep. A pulsating machine pours oxygen from a hollow hose into Rachael's mouth.

Eerie shadows form on the ceiling above the nurse's desk lamp.

There is no bed locker. People who stay in this

cubicle have little need for perfumed toiletries or spotty flannel nighties folded on warm slippers. White cotton gowns that open at the back are the uniform.

The room is kept cool. The red-haired nurse wears a white hospital gown over the blue scrubs for warmth.

The family scrutinizes the nurse; she is in perpetual motion. She records blood pressure, pulse, and temperature, then regulates the machinery around Rachael. She measures urine levels, takes blood gases. The nurse shines a torch into Rachael's unresponsive eyes. The details are recorded on a large sheet of paper stretching across the small table. Every so often, the nurse enters notes on the computer.

The nurse has a one-sided conversation with Rachael and is not troubled by the lack of response.

"Rachael, I am about to remove the secretions in your throat. You will hear a noise and feel a sucking sensation; it will last only a few seconds."

The suction sound reverberates through the cubicle.

"I'm taking blood from your intravenous line," she said. "Can you hear me? Squeeze my hand if you can. I'm shining a torch in your eyes. Can you see the light? Are you in pain?"

The others in the room are wallflowers to this elaborate healing dance.

Two female doctors walk into the room; they

also shine a torch in Rachael's eyes. They speak softly and make inaudible calculations.

"Nurse, I altered the medication," One doctor said.

"When will Rachael come out of the coma?" asked Paula to the doctor.

"It is very difficult to predict a time," said the Registrar.

"Rachael sustained a nasty right leg fracture and, more disturbing, damage to the frontal lobe of the brain." The doctor lets the words sink in.

"Unfortunately, the pressure in Rachael's brain is increasing, and her uneven pupils suggest a possible brain haemorrhage."

She stops. "The next forty-eight hours will be vital to your daughter's survival."

Paula, Colin, and Sarah know it means Rachael may die. Despite the machines, regardless of the intensive ward staff, even the nurses' healing dance with the equipment. Despite everything.

The three cling to a dream, a miracle.

They are entrenched with the machinery, breathing in rhythm as one with the paraphernalia in the cubicle.

There are invisible ghosts of others who previously lay in this same bed. A number survived; some did not.

Death prowls on the edges.

Fear pervades.

A tsunami of distress rolls over, submerging everyone.

~

Only hours ago, Rachael peddled her bicycle to school. It might have been days, or minutes. Time has lost significance. Rachael was smashed by a P-plate driver going too fast. She was flung over the windscreen, cracking the glass before slipping unconscious to the road.

~

No one ever imagines waiting in an intensive care ward. When it occurs, it slews life out of the living. They are powerless and sentient to this second and the next moment. Paula, Colin, and Sarah grip onto a scrap of hope.

The three are now seared with the imprint of this room, this situation. It is tattooed on their DNA, scorching something different in each. They are transformed and altered. Each will carry the brokenness. They will never feel safe again. Always holding their breath for the dreaded other shoe to drop.

This morning, life was predictable.

Now they have become aliens, extraterrestrials, detached from the rest of humanity who are living regular lives.

A radiology machine rolls in. They move to one

side of the room as images are taken of a brain leaking blood which is swelling, pushing, and distorting Rachael's brain.

Rachael does not call out in pain.

Her small arms outstretched on the white sheet. The broken leg elevated on a bolster.

The nurse touches Paula's arm gently; she suggests the family wait outside.

"Have a cup of tea. The waiting room has sandwiches and biscuits. While you are gone, I will sponge Rachael, change the sheets and make her comfortable. Come back in half an hour."

Paula links arms with Sarah, they move as one. Colin lags staring back at Rachael.

A dark-skinned woman stands at the far corner of the tea room; she leans against the wall. She wears a blue scarf on her head, her dark fingers clamped in prayer.

The two women's eyes connect. Terror meets distress.

Paula acknowledges the woman and nods. The woman gestures back.

The small fridge whirs. A white dishtowel folded on top. This small machine has been privy to furtive conversations related to bloodied sufferers of criminality, violence, and trauma. It preserves the secrets; hums to itself.

Colin glares at the wall. Paula clutches her bag on her lap. No one speaks.

Sarah assembles three generic tea bags and

paper cups. Pours scalding water, inspects the clotted stale milk, and throws the cups into the bin.

Paula folds scraps of thoughts in her head related to the missing ribbon.

Did I thread one ribbon in her hair this morning?

She remembers she shouted at Rachael, who as usual dawdled over breakfast.

"Hurry up, you will be late for school," Paula had said.

Somewhere in the corridor running feet echo past, then the screech of carts dragging. Then the sound of doors opening and slamming.

Then silence.

"It is half an hour," said Sarah.

They move back to the ward.

The endotracheal tube is still strapped to the small mouth. Rachael's position has been altered. She is surrounded by crisp, clean, white sheets. The blood smear has vanished. Her right leg still elevated.

The equipment vibrates; emits swooshing gurgles. It is the guardian of Rachael's soul, holding on by a slender thread to prevent her from slipping away.

"Take Sarah home; she needs to sleep. I will stay here," said Paula.

Colin and Sarah reluctantly leave.

Paula closes her eyes.

She rouses with a jerk, uncertain where she is.

Finds a pen, scrawls a list on the back of an envelope.

"Notify Rachael's school, notify my work, tell my parents."

Paula watches the nurse glide around Rachael.

I can't breathe, I need to get out.

She opens the door of the Intensive Care Unit ward, stands in the corridor gulping air.

She sends a text message to Jenny; they have been close friends since university days. Straight away there is a response.

The blue light of the mobile phone flicks on and off. Soundless words soar from the Parkville room to a small flat in Carlton and back. Connections and comfort shared via networks.

When she returns to Rachael's cubicle, two doctors and the nurse are huddled around the monitors, deliberating over medical reports.

Paula is cognizant of other men and women in other cubicles. She notices the woman with the scarf is in the adjoining booth.

The registrar moves to Paula.

"The scan confirms a hematoma, a bleed to the right side of the brain."

"We have booked the theatre, Rachael will be operated on now," the doctor said, uneasiness in his voice. "Rachael's hair will be shaved. We will open the skull and stop the bleeding. A metal rod will be inserted into her broken femur."

Paula looks blank inability to take it in. She repeats the words to herself.

They intend to shave Rachael's head, open her skull...

Her hand shakes as she signs the consent form. Paula is gap-mouthed, attempting to take it in, to recollect the essentials.

She bends over her unmoving daughter.

"Rachael, sweetheart, they are going to take you to surgery to fix your leg, and..."

Paula cannot go on. She kisses her daughter's cheek.

"Everything will be fine, love you...," her voice a hoarse whisper.

Abruptly she turns to the nurse. "Can I have the yellow ribbon from Rachael's pigtail?"

The nurse nods, removes the ribbon, and hands it to her.

Paula runs trembling fingers over the fabric lengthwise, smooths, traces the red, raised spots in the pattern, caresses, and then puts it to her lips. Rolls and unrolls the ribbon.

She watches the orderlies steer the bed to the operating room.

She waits in the empty cubicle.

The red-haired nurse leads Paula to a tiny room devoid of all furniture, except a bed.

"Stay here, try to sleep. If you need anything, call me," said the nurse. "The minute Rachael's back from recovery I will come and get you," the nurse said. "Hang onto whatever makes you strong."

Paula rings Colin with the recent update.

"Poor Rachael," his voice incoherent, he is crying again.

"Rachael is in good hands," she whispers, but cannot continue.

One of us must be strong.

"Please, bring my toilet bag, stockings, underpants, and a warm cardigan when you come."

Paula stares out of the window, a wash of pink moves across the lightening horizon. Paula throws her black coat on the bed.

∼

Paula purchased the black coat at a Myer sale five years ago. She grabbed the coat regardless of the vocal disapproval of another shopper.

"I saw the coat first," said the woman.

"It is too big for you," said Paula and marched, head held high to the counter.

The black coat was too large for Paula as well, but she didn't care. It had wonderful deep pockets. Paula relished shoving her hands down, retrieving crumpled tissues and small coins. The coat allowed her to merge into the background. Sarah calls the coat "the Stormtroopers coat." It carries an aroma of stale Arpege perfume. It is now shabby. Fluff gathers on the wool. The lining unravelled at the hem. Paula knows she should take it to a charity shop. The third button is loose. She forgets to mend it, remembering when she next buttons the coat.

∼

Paula stands at the window and remembers a sleepless night years ago when Rachael was four months old and Paula twenty-three.

That night the sky had a golden tinge that broke out of the inky darkness. She held the baby wrapped in a pink flannel rug with laughing yellow rabbits around the edge. The baby had been crying non-stop despite being changed, fed, and burped. The baby's cry rose and fell, a curtain flapping in the wind. Dark hair matted with sweat. The face crumpled. Tiny fingers and legs flailed with the screaming. Cheeks burning red, tongue moving in sync like a metronome.

Paula had turned on the radio.

Leonard Cohen sang a song about a bird on a wire.

The baby gave a snuffle and stopped crying.

"I see you are a Leonard Cohen fan."

When the song ended, the infant cried again. Paula searched for a CD and crooned with the music.

The singer sang about waiting for a miracle to come.

Tiny fingers gripped Paula's thumb, yawned and closed her eyes.

"You will never be a stranger to me," Paula said.

～

Today Paula lies on the bed and draws the coat over her feet. The door is ajar. Electric floor polishers vibrate in the corridor, cleaners talk.

THREE

Spiders
November 2001, Parkville

RACHAEL SENSES A BLAZE OF SILVER SPARKLING, IT vanishes, then nothingness. A whiff of asphalt, stifled thuds dangle in the air.

Where am I?

Her thoughts freeze. She feels a fluttering in her stomach.

She hears a voice from far away.

"Rachel, can you hear me?"

Who is that? Why are they calling my name?

Rachael feels pressure on her hand.

What was that?

She attempts to open her eyelids.

"Rachael, squeeze my hand," said a voice.

Rachael's heart beats faster, her breathing increases.

Go away.

"Rachael is back," said the nurse to the family.

Paula, Colin, and Sarah gather around Rachael's bed, shouting in excitement.

The nurse removes the breathing tube.

A shaft of light warms the room.

Rachael's eyes flicker.

"Hello, darling, how are you?" Paula's voice trembles.

"Dad's here," Colin bellows.

He blows his nose on a large white handkerchief. A smile festooned on his face. He bounces back on forth on his feet.

"Rachael, it's me, Sarah." Sarah held herself taut for days, afraid to let go, now she releases the tension, breathes out.

Rachael's eyes linger over the strange forms, as if in a mist.

Nothing makes sense.

Rachael floats in and out of consciousness. She has a sense of being covered by terrifying black spiders. She tries to escape the hairy beasts, yells, and lashes around in bed.

"Does your leg hurt?" asked the nurse bending over to Rachael.

"Nutmeg...nutmeg...nutmeg."

"Why does she say nutmeg?" Colin's face creases into a frown. He turns and looks at the doctor standing behind them.

"Rachael is experiencing Post-Traumatic Amnesia or PTA. The severity and length of time it continues is indicative of the damage to the brain," said the doctor.

He struggles to find the appropriate words, taps a finger against his lip.

"Rachael's conscious. That's good, isn't? The

broken bone will mend and so will her brain," Colin said. His face is full of optimism.

He notices the doctor does not answer. A sudden heaviness descends upon Colin and runs a hand over his head.

"It will take time; that is to be expected. Perhaps she can return to school in a month." Colin's voice is questioning, begging for affirmation.

The doctor soothes his shirt and locates a pen. After a pause, he chooses his words with care.

"Rachael will not be as before. Right now, she needs as much support and love as you can give." He pauses again. "Let's see what extensive rehabilitation can do."

FOUR

Juxtaposing the new Rachael with the old
November 2001

WHEN RACHAEL IS STABLE, SHE IS MOVED TO A specialist rehabilitation unit. She struggles with speech and memory. Cannot weight-bear on the broken leg, needs to be wheeled everywhere. A large white scar is noticeable on her skull and tufts of soft dark hair advance over her bald head.

Paula compares this person to the daughter she knew. This new person has terrors and screaming outbursts, throws whatever is within reach, then cries without stopping.

I want my old Rachael back.

School friends visit. They clasp chocolates and handwritten get-well cards. Rachael's tantrums frighten them. After a time, they stop visiting.

"She'll return to school next semester." Colin remains confident. But his voice is low-pitched and tightens his fists. Muscles clench along his jaw. He holds a frozen smile.

Paula stares at her nails. She pushes her sleeves up. Inhales. Feels a headache coming.

At home, Sarah gathers the family's washing from the clothesline, prepares simple meals, runs errands. One day she nicks her finger with the curved nail scissors while trimming her nails. Blood trickle through her fingers, feels warm. Repeats the cutting and the warm sensation follows.

FIVE

Unexploded bombs
December 2001

EVERY DAY IS A MINEFIELD. UNEXPLODED BOMBS HIDE under the surface. Everything is turmoil and compromise. Daily, Colin and Paula drive to the rehabilitation centre to check on Rachael's progress. They clutch handwritten tasks for the day.

'Meet with the medical team. Work with Rachael with physiotherapy and speech therapy.'

"It might be better if you weren't so involved in Rachael's treatment," said the speech pathologist.

"We want to give our daughter the best chance at rehabilitation." Colin said. He places hands in his pockets and stands firm. Privately, he is troubled, Rachael is not improving. One moment Rachael clutches at them not letting go.

"Please stay with me, I'm scared," Rachael sobs.

This is followed by a tirade of abuse.

"I hate you. Leave me alone."

"Brains need time to mend," Colin said, gritting his teeth.

Paula places clammy hands in her pocket, holds back a comment.

I wonder if Rachael's problems are permanent. The tantrums exhaust me. Colin insists I go with him.

They watch Rachael lift a spoon with the scrambled eggs to her mouth. The egg falls on her chest.

"Bum," Rachael shouts. She picks up the yellow plastic plate and throws it at her father. "I hate you."

"Rachael…" Colin said. He brushes the yellow mixture from his shirt.

"Come on, you can do it. Try again." His voice has an annoyed edge.

"I need a coffee. Do you want one?" asked Paula

Paula leaves the room ignoring Colin's black looks.

She stands near the front entrance of the hospital. Small birds peck at insects in the grass. Every so often the sun shines through the clouds.

This is another world.

She watches a girl in a wheelchair play catch with a therapist.

Paula locates the coffee shop, orders a latte. She notices a familiar face the corner.

It's the woman with the blue scarf from the intensive care ward.

She goes to the woman, touches her shoulder. "Excuse me," said Paula.

The woman jumps.

"I didn't mean to startle you," Paula said.

"I remember you from the intensive care ward when I was there with my daughter. You were in the next cubicle to ours."

Can I sit with you?" asked Paula.

"How is your husband?"

"My husband," the woman shakes her head, "he is like a child."

The woman gives a heavy sigh.

"How can I live?"

She stops and surveys the window.

"We left our country because of the war. I am fighting another battle here."

There is a thickness in her throat.

"I have two young children." She holds a tissue to her mouth.

"Every day I come here. My friend cares for the children. But my husband, he is not…my husband. He is a stranger, excuse my English." She fiddles with the menu on the table.

"Your English is fine," said Paula.

"When a child is hurt it's terrible," the lady continues in a burst.

"But when the father is damaged, how can you feed the children?" She stops.

"Do you want a coffee?" Paula said.

"I have no money."

Paula buys coffee and a muffin.

"Eat." Paula puts the food in front of the woman.

"Everything is different when you have food in your stomach."

Paula leans forward. "Have you seen the social worker? She can organise a pension for you."

The woman shakes her head. She breaks the muffin into small pieces.

"How is your daughter?"

"The girl in my daughter's body is no one I know. I keep asking myself where is the old Rachael? Will she ever come back?" asked Paula.

She glances at her watch, stands up.

"I should return to the ward. My husband will wonder what happened to me."

Paula takes a $50 from her purse and folds it into the woman's hand.

"Please buy food for the children until you have the carer's pension."

"God bless you and your daughter." The woman closes her fingers around the money. Her scarf entangles around Paula's neck chain. Wisps of black hair slip out. She rearranges it back under her scarf.

Rachael is laughing when Paula returns to the ward. Colin squats on the floor, he is doing a version of a chicken dance, elbows out as wings.

"You were a long time buying coffee," he said straightening.

She ignores his comment.

"Let's both steer the food and try to land it in your mouth."

She laces her fingers around Rachael's small ones. Four teaspoons of yogurt make it into Rachael's mouth.

SIX

Mrs Gilbert
December 2001

FRIDAY AFTERNOON, PAULA WAITS OUTSIDE SARAH'S school.

"How's Rachael?" asked Mrs Gilbert, the form teacher.

"She's improving every day," said Paula, this is her stock answer.

"Good. I want to talk to you." Mrs Gilbert drops her voice to a whisper. "Have you noticed Sarah has lost weight?"

Paula is shocked, quickly regains her composure.

"Sarah's fine-boned like me." Paula's cheeks flame. "She's fine." Is about to say something nasty but bits her tongue. "Thank you for your concern." *Who the hell does this woman think she is?*

That night at dinner, Paula watches Sarah cut a sausage into small pieces. She makes a pile of the mashed potato and beans, moves them to one side. It looks as she has eaten half the food on her plate.

This is odd. Thinks Paula.

Sarah looks up and notices her mother watching.

"I'm not hungry. Tracey and I shared a cheeseburger and chips after school."

The story sounds convincing, even the part related to Tracey going back for more chips. However, Tracey was in Brisbane holidaying with her family at the time.

SEVEN

Strange weather
December 2001

LAST NIGHT, PAULA DREAMT SHE WORE THE PINK, frothy dress with the two stiff, white petticoats that Aunt Bertha made for her eighth birthday. It had a swirling skirt and blue sash.

When she wakes she shivers uncontrollably, has a feeling of intense fear in her gut. She goes to the window.

It's such strange weather. The leaves of the roses are dry and withered.

EIGHT

Colin and the call from the rehabilitation hospital
February 2002

THE UTILITY SKITTERS TO A STOP. COLIN PUMPS THE horn at a bent old man creeps snail-like across the pedestrian crossing.

"Come on, move it," Colin said, toots the horn again.

The old man brandishes a walking stick at Colin's utility.

"I'll smash your car headlights," he said.

Thinks better of it and moves to the footpath.

Colin speeds up and suddenly slams the brakes, ahead is a towering cattle-truck the width of the road. It looms ahead blocking his vision.

Bloody hell, that was close.

He trails the truck for ten minutes, edges the utility to the right planning to overtake, jerks back when he sees an oncoming car.

"Keep calm," Colin said out loud. Sweat beads grow on his forehead.

Colin's car follows the truck as it snakes around bends, pass eucalyptus trees and green pastures and now and then a cow, a house here and there in the distance.

Colin flicks the radio on. It crackles, and he flips the stations reaching for better reception.

"My beans have black spots. What could cause this?" asked a female voice.

"It might be mould. How often do you water?" The announcer replied.

"I'm free with the watering," she giggles.

"Bloody fool." Colin changes the station.

"The string quartet will now play Bach's B Minor."

Colin's feels his neck become hot; he pounds a fist against the dashboard.

Cows peer out of the truck's metal railings, sad and mournful. The animals are jammed tight next to each other to prevent them from falling. They sway and stumble trying to keep their balance. Every so often a cow lets out a gut-wrenching moo. The stench of manure filters through Colin's utility.

Poor devils.

Colin edges out again ready to overtake the truck. A white van toots warning from the opposite direction as it passes. A huge raindrop crashes into the windshield, followed by another, it starts to pour. The windscreen wipers struggle to cope, one screeches in a noisy arc. He clutches the wheel, shadows the cattle truck around bends and turns. He turns the radio back on.

"These are the current traffic hazards. Flash flooding has caused the closure of the Calder Highway from Kyneton to Sunbury turnoff," said the radio announcer.

"Please take alternative routes. A five-car pileup near Bulla Hill, be prepared for long delays."

"Damn!"

Colin pulls into a bus shelter. He dials Paula's mobile. The phone rings out. *Where the hell is she?*

The rain eases. White cockatoos screech as they fly past. Colin taps the steering wheel. He decides to ring Paula's mother Doris at her nursing home.

∼

Doris once lived with Paula's family after her husband Stan died.

Rachael's accident created an opportunity for a nursing home bed for Doris on compassionate grounds. Doris hates the nursing home.

"The nurses are harsh and cruel. The food's a sloppy mess. I am here in this horrid place because my daughter refuses to care for me," she tells anyone who will listen.

Paula's brother, Daniel, and wife, Julia, visit. They can't deal with Doris's endless complaints and devise elaborate excuses not to visit.

"Sorry, Mum. We can't come in tomorrow as the cat needs to go to the vet. The heater is on the blink and we are waiting for the repairman," Daniel said.

It is left to Paula to squeeze in visits to Doris between times caring for Rachael.

~

"Is Mrs Paula Wilson visiting Doris Parker? I am her husband. Tell her I must speak with her." Colin's voice growls with urgency.

After a short time, Paula comes to the phone. "What's the matter? I'm with Mother."

"Rachael's having an anxiety attack. I was on my way to seeing her, but the road is blocked near Gisborne. Can you drop what you are doing and see her?" Colin said. He tugs at his eyebrow.

Paula sighs.

At least once a week he panics over something related to Rachael.

"I am not up for Rachael's tantrums today. Anyway, I have an academic meeting tonight." She plucks threads from her skirt.

"Cancel the bloody meeting!" Colin balls his fists.

"I'll ring the hospital to see what is going on," she said.

"Rachael's asleep," said the charge nurse. Paula relays the news to Colin.

"Are you telling me you refuse to go to her?" His words spit out.

"Caving into Rachael every time she misbehaves is unproductive."

"Paula," as though speaking to a child, "our daughter has sustained head injuries and has a wretched life, can't you—?"

"All right...all right."

"And keep your phone switched on," he said.

Paula returns to Doris, who sits on the walker, dunking a Marie biscuit in a cup of tea.

"Mother, I have to go. Something has come up with Rachael," said Paula, bends to kiss her goodbye.

"That girl has all your attention. What about me?"

It's always about you.

Paula strides down the hall.

"Mrs Wilson," the Director of Nursing calls. "Please come to the office."

She motions Paula to sit.

What has Mother done now?

"Your mother has threatened to hit another resident again. It's obvious she is unhappy here and takes it out on the others."

Paula takes short breaths to gain control. "Can't you give her something to sedate her?"

"We use behavioural management here," said the Director of Nursing.

She coughs, tries to find the right words.

"Mrs Parker hasn't responded well to our routines. There have been several complaints by the other residents and their families." Pauses; shuffles some papers on her desk.

"We've been patient. I understand your family has pressing issues with your daughter and her accident...." Moves the papers back where they were.

"Four weeks should be enough time to find a more suitable nursing home for your mother."

Paula closes her eyes.

My mother is determined to make my life a misery.

~

It's a slow trip to the rehabilitation centre; the peak hour traffic reduces the traffic flow to a crawl. Sometime later Paula arrives at Rachael's room to find her in deep sleep.

Family photos are arranged on the brown corkboard behind the bed. One photo shows Rachael with an arm around Sarah's shoulder, another with friends, and other standing with Colin at the beach.

Paula stares at the photo and remembers the beach with the row of striped red-and-blue beach towels flapping on the line.

There was always a yellow film of sand covering the floor of the beach house. I can almost smell the sunblock and how it stained bathers.

Doris used to doze on the navy deck chair under the green beach umbrella on the water's edge. Every so often Doris would call 'While you're up, get me a nice drink.' Later, Doris would tuck the floral dress in white bloomers and paddle in the shallows.

Rachael never feared my dragon Mother.

～

Paula recalls Rachael's strident voice calling Colin to join her in the sea.

"Too freezing," he said. Colin wore the ripped, blue towelling hat that he used to stick his fingers through the holes.

"It is ventilation for my brain," he said.

"Come on, Dad!" yelled Rachael, jumping up and down in the water.

Eventually, Colin dipped his toe in the water. "Freezing," he said.

"Just dive in, Dad."

He dive-bombed into the water, disturbed the squawking seagulls. Swam to *The Ozone*, grabbed the wooden wheel of the abounded boat, and waved to the others on the beach. Later Colin constructed a platform with two hands, Rachael used it to lurch into the water, shrieking with laughter.

They returned to the beach umbrella dripping wet and exhilarated.

That was so long ago.

～

Today, a soft toy dog with bulging eyes hangs on a metal handgrip above Rachael's bed. Four worn get-well cards lean against the water jug.

Paula scans the day's activities board. Most of the day is scheduled with appointments such as physiotherapy and occupational therapy.

No wonder she gets frustrated.

The tea lady knocks.

"Would Rachael like a drink?"

"She's asleep," she said nodding towards her bed.

"Then you can have a hot cup of tea and a biscuit," said the tea lady handing her a cup.

Paula writes in Rachael's communication book. "Visited you at 6:30 p.m. but found you dreaming. love Mother xx."

She collects Rachael's soiled clothes from the cupboard.

"Why was Rachael so difficult today?" Paula asked the receptionist.

"She refused to go to speech therapy; screamed for ages," she said.

"I nearly forgot, I have a note for you." The receptionist picks up a folded note, reads it to Paula.

"The next family meeting for Rachael Wilson is on Friday at 2 p.m. Topic for discussion is Rachael's discharge. The occupational therapist has completed the home inspection. Handrails and grab bars have been fitted in the bathroom and toilet."

She glances at Paula.

"Does Friday suit you?"

"We'll be there."

~

When Paula arrives home, Colin is in his usual place in front of the television.

"How's Rachael?"

"She was asleep when I arrived and didn't wake. I think they gave her something to calm her down."

She fishes the note from her bag.

"We have to attend a parents' meeting on Friday at two o'clock. The rehabilitation staff feels she is ready for home discharge. I understand she will continue with outpatient rehabilitation. A rehab van will take her to rehab and back."

Her heart thumps loudly; she is sure he can hear it. "They need her bed for a new acute client."

She finishes speaking and sits. The colour has drained from her face. "I am not sure I can cope."

"She's nowhere near ready to come home," he said, interrupting her. "I don't think she is ready to come home..." he said.

Paula stares at the wall.

"The nursing home wants to kick Doris out. She threatened to hit another resident again." Her face is expressionless.

"If Doris is angling to come back here, tell her that is not an option." he said. "It will be hard enough for us with Rachael here." He checks himself.

Paula shrugs her shoulders. They sit in silence.

"Where's Sarah?" she said.

"She is upstairs working on a science project about the exoplanets."

Paula climbs the stairs, pulling at the rails as she climbs. She knocks on Sarah's door.

"Hello, Sweetheart."

Paula gives Sarah a long hug. "How was your day?"

Several textbooks are spread out on the bed, a pile of papers on the desk.

Paula picks up a poster of the solar system.

"It looks as if you are right into the science project." Paula sits on the bed.

"How would you feel if Rachael came home soon?"

Sarah hesitates, blinks, peers at the computer screen, and then taps on the computer mouse. Turns to her mother, is about to say something but stops, shrugs her shoulders.

"I did the washing," said Sarah.

"You're an angel. Thank you."

Downstairs a phone rings.

"Paula, call for you," calls Colin.

She goes downstairs.

"Mrs Parker refuses to go to bed, demands you

come in and see her," said the agitated voice of a nurse.

In the background, Doris could be heard shouting, "Tell Paula she must come in and see me now."

"Tell her I visited earlier." Paula hangs up the phone.

I am being squeezed tight by everyone's needs.

NINE

Jenny
March 2002, Kensington

EARLIER IN THE DAY, PAULA RANG JENNY.

"Can you please stay with Rachael while Colin and I attend a meeting? I know it is short notice," said Paula.

"Of course," said Jenny.

Jenny parks her red Mazda outside the house on Westbourne Road. She smooths her dark cropped hair, straightens the tight red jumper over blue jeans and frowns.

I wonder what's going on.

Paula's home is the same on the outside. The lawns are trimmed; along the tidy edges are borders of pink petunias. The gum tree is covered in flowers.

Jenny pushes the doorbell. No answer.

She rings again. "Hello, is anyone home?"

She bangs on the door.

Paula flings the door open; she is still in her dressing gown. She glances up the street as though she's looking for someone. Without speaking grabs

Jenny's arm and pulls her inside the house and leans against the closed front door.

Paula is aware that Jenny is staring at her.

"It has been a difficult few days," Paula said.

Jenny notices that dirty wine glasses are stacked on the sink. Plates with pieces of toast sit on the table. Paula's black coat dangles off the back of a chair, several pairs of shoes kicked to the side.

A wailing noise, like a wounded animal, drifts from upstairs.

Paula looks up towards the room.

"That's Rachael; she's vocalizing. You will get used to the sound," said Paula.

She runs fingers through her tangled uncombed hair.

"Thanks for coming at such short notice."

"You look so worried. I can manage," said Jenny.

She gives a half-hearted laugh.

"I work with disturbed adolescents every day, I think I can manage Rachael for one afternoon."

Things must be terrible.... Paula in a dressing gown at this time of day...the house in a mess.

"Do you want a cup of coffee?" asked Paula.

No, you and Colin get ready for your meeting."

Paula hesitates.

"Try to be calm. Don't shout. Rachael will do enough shouting."

"We'll be back in less than two hours."

She gives Jenny a spontaneous hug.

"Thank you."

Jenny almost trips on a damp towel on the top stairs. Takes a deep breath, knocks on Rachael's door, no answer, and gingerly opens it.

Rachael is crouching on the floor, a flowered pink and white doona draped around her shoulders. She clutches a large brown teddy.

"Hello Rachael," said Jenny, bending over as if to kiss her. "What are you doing here?" Rachael glares at Jenny. "Where's my Mother?"

"I'm keeping you company while your parents are out."

"I don't want to see you. Go away."

Rachael hurls a picture book, then two cushions and a hairbrush at Jenny. All of them miss.

"I want my father." Rachael's voice is hysterical. "I want my father!"

She tosses the teddy at Jenny who ducks. It hits the window and it splinters into pieces. Small window fragments cascade on the carpet. Rachael treads on a slither of glass and the peach carpet develops a bright red gash.

"Your mother will not be happy if you bleed on her carpet," said Jenny,

She heaves Rachael onto the bed.

"Go away. I hate you. I want my mother." Rachael punches Jenny.

"Bad luck; your mother isn't here."

What the heck do I do now? Think, think…

"Once upon a time…" starts Jenny in a loud voice, still holding the wriggling girl. "There lived a princess called Rachael, who had a birthday at the zoo-"

"That's a stupid baby story," said Rachael.

Jenny continues in a loud sing-song voice.

"The birthday girl laughed at the pelicans marching around the pool. They took turns diving off the tallest rock and ended in the water. Splat!" Jenny emphasizes with a thick clap.

"The penguins splashed the onlookers, drenching them. Men, women, boys, and girls had water dripping off their noses." Jenny gives a hyena laugh. "The lion roared," Jenny growls.

"The elephants trumpeted." Jenny made a horn sound.

"The animals laughed. The sentry meerkat stood as a statue on top of a large rock. He was always on guard."

Rachel is silent.

"The baby meerkats played chase around the rocks; one hid in a cave." Jenny used two fingers to show him hiding.

"Princess Rachael went to the Butterfly House. She stood still as a meerkat sentry. Three blue and yellow butterflies landed on her head." Jenny becomes a statue and lowers her voice.

"Do you remember I had a special zoo pass and used to take you and Sarah to the zoo as often as we wanted? Your mother never came to the zoo with us; she couldn't bear to see the animals locked in cages."

Rachael sits motionless.

"Do you remember the year we had your birthday at Luna Park? The dodgem cars were your favourite; you had six rides. I had to drag you off."

Rachael nodded.

"And the ghost train…" said Rachael.

"Oh yes. I yelled my head off when the vampire leapt out of the dark."

"You said, 'Shit, shit.'"

A smile spreads over Rachael's face.

"And you begged us not to tell Mother you swore."

Jenny grinned, "Your mother hates swearing."

She considers Rachael's face. "We should go to Luna Park again. It must be horrible being stuck in the house."

"Am I a freak?" asked Rachael.

"Why? Would you say that? How can you be a freak? You are my gorgeous goddaughter."

Jenny puts her arms out. "Come and give me a cuddle. It is ages since I had a decent hug from you."

Two hours later, Paula and Colin return home and are unnerved by the quiet. They open the bedroom door softly. Jenny is curled up next to Rachael, reading a book. A soft breeze blows from the broken window. The contents from the bookshelf piled in a corner.

"Was there an earthquake?" Colin said.

"A small Rachael earthquake; four on the Richter scale," said Jenny.

TEN

Mrs Gilbert and Sarah
April 2002

"Sarah, please stay after class," said Mrs Gilbert.

Tracey glances at Sarah, who makes a face.

English literature classes are finished; the air is stifling hot. It's been a long, tedious day for students and teacher alike. The other students leave.

Outside the classroom the sharp afternoon sun is still hot.

Sarah moves towards the teacher's desk, trailing her heavy backpack.

"Sit down," nods Mrs Gilbert. She recognises fear in Sarah's face. "You haven't done anything wrong. I wanted to talk to you."

She sucks her bottom lip and brushes invisible strands of hair from her face.

"I'm aware your family is having a few problems after Rachael's terrible bike accident."

Sarah fidgets.

It is always about Rachael.

"Are you all right?" asked Mrs Gilbert.

"I am okay," said Sarah, her voice sharp, stares at the dust on her shoes.

"I'm sure you are on the surface. Rachael's accident must have changed your life. A family member with head injuries can be destabilizing." She takes a breath.

"My brother Frank sustained head injuries when he fell off a horse. I remember how crazy life was for the family and for Frank." She takes off her glasses, cleans them.

"Did Frank have Post-Traumatic Amnesia?" asked Sarah.

"That term was not used in those days. Probably he did. But he was angry and disruptive. Frank punched holes in his bedroom wall in frustration."

"What happened to him?"

"He moved out. The truth is, Father threw him out." Mrs Gilbert stares at the ceiling. "Frank died a year later."

"Did he kill himself?" Sarah's cheeks are burning red. "Rachael threatens to kill herself all the time."

Sarah covers her mouth.

"Yes," Mrs Gilbert said, her voice became very soft. "After the accident, he felt an outsider. It broke my heart to see him like that."

She removes her glasses and wipes her eyes.

"I had a wonderful cousin who lived in the country. She took me to her farm." Mrs Gilbert stops, stares unblinking at the back wall.

"I threw stones into the dam until my arms

ached." She holds the desk. "I'm not sure why I'm telling you this." Mrs Gilbert scrutinises the desk.

"I wanted you to know I am here for you. And I understand."

Outside in the schoolyard, a mobile phone rang.

"If you want to get anything off your chest, see me, or a school counsellor can be arranged."

Sarah does not speak.

"You can go now," said Mrs Gilbert.

Mrs Gilbert sharpens three pencils, lines them side by side, and arranges them by colour, thickness, and length. With a flourish, she shoves them in the desk drawer and slams it shut.

Sarah drags her school bag, climbs the steps to the front door.

"That must be the weirdest conversation I have ever had with a teacher. No way am I going to any stupid counsellor," said Sarah to herself.

Rachael's screams pour from the upstairs window.

"No, no, no. You can't make me," said Rachael.

"Come on Rachael," pleads Colin.

Sarah hides in the pantry and nibbles two dry Salada biscuits. She makes them last a long time. She licks the crumbs from her fingers. Goes to the sink and drinks three glasses of water.

ELEVEN

Sarah and Rachael
July 2002, Kensington

A SOUND LIKE A FLUTTERING WHEEL OF A MACHINE starts and then stops. Sarah puts down her book. It starts again.

What now with the drama queen?

She goes to Rachael's room.

"Rachael, why are you making such a din?"

Rachel is in her usual position on the floor, a doona around her body like a tent.

Sarah rolls her eyes. She lifts the doona next to Rachael.

"What's the matter little sister?"

"I'm lost. I can't think straight," said Rachael.

"You'll get better," Sarah puts her arms around her and gives her a squeeze. "Dad said it takes time."

"My leg's better but my brain doesn't work," said Rachael.

"Brains take longer."

"People call me a weirdo," said Rachael.

"No, they don't."

"The boy next door calls me a freak."

"You scare people with your screaming," Sarah said.

"I spilled orange juice on the carpet yesterday. Mother told me off and said I had to learn to be careful." She looked at Sarah. "I didn't do it on purpose."

"Mother is fussy about the house; you know that. Don't take it personally."

At that moment Colin bursts in, he carries a shoe box with small air holes and places it on the carpet.

"Is this a special sister moment? Can a father gate crash?" He peers under the doona.

The girls motion him to join them.

"Two gorgeous girls," he said.

"One small girl and one big. If you promise not to shout, I have a surprise."

He places a box on Rachael's knees.

"Open it."

Rachael fumbles with the box and lets out a loud squeal. Inside is a brown tortoise, a piece of string trailing from the hole in the shell.

"A tortoise," said Sarah.

"Where did you find him?"

"Actually, he found me. He came into our garden looking for adventure."

The tortoise pokes a wrinkled neck out of the shell.

"Hello," said Rachael.

"I'm not sure what he eats, we can chase up the

information. I think Toddles is a good name," said Colin.

"That's a terrible name. Let's call him Doris after grandma," said Rachael, grinning. "She is always sticking her nose into things."

"He's a boy tortoise, and I don't think your mother would like a tortoise named after her mother. But I can see he does look a bit like your grandmother," he smiles.

"Ok, Doris it is. We can build a hutch, so he doesn't escape again. I'm going to check my garage for usable timber." He hurries out.

The girls watch the tortoise as he moves around the floor.

"Sarah, I still see scary spiders," said Rachael.

"Are they hairy ones or smiling happy ones?"

"They are horrible black spiders with nasty, beady eyes."

"Yuck. Is that why you scream?" asked Sarah.

"They're on Mother's hands sometimes."

"Are they on me?"

"Spiders are afraid of you."

"My teacher told me when her brother fell off a horse and hurt his head, he imagined frightening things too. He punched a hole in the bedroom wall," said Sarah.

"Did he get better?"

"Not sure," Sarah's voices trails.

"When your brain heals, the spiders will go away."

"Will people stop calling me a freak then?" asked Rachael.

"You're not a freak."

Sarah pulls the two pillows off the bed. They make a tent under the doona.

"No spiders here," said Sarah. "This is a spider-free zone."

"No spiders here," repeats Rachael.

"Call me when you see them. I will smash them away," she said, chopping the side of the doona.

When Paula calls them for dinner they are in the tent. A curious Doris-tortoise looks at her.

TWELVE

The hospital appointment
July 2002, Parkville

IT IS FIVE MONTHS SINCE RACHAEL'S DISCHARGE FROM the rehabilitation unit. The family has learned to deal with uncertainty and has carved up the family responsibilities. They have a solid system going. Paula works in the afternoon at the university. This enables Colin to work in the garage in the mornings. Paula does the hospital and doctor appointments with Rachael, which are mostly in the mornings. In the afternoon while Paula is at work, Colin prepares lunch and entertains Rachel.

They all share the evening chores, cooking, and showering. Supervise Rachael's exercises at night and the excruciating task of getting her to bed. She dawdles and puts off going to bed with all her might.

Sarah keeps to her schoolwork and friends and assists when necessary.

Every second Saturday, Jenny comes to the house and stays with Rachael.

During those times, Paula and Sarah rush to a movie at Highpoint and make hasty stabs at shopping.

Colin has a few beers with friends.

Alternate Sundays, Colin's Brother Max and his wife Barbara collect Rachael and take her to their home to play computer games with their son Trevor.

Today Paula and Rachael are at the neurology clinic. The waiting room is cramped with people, some wearing bandaged heads. Others have plastered limbs extended on chairs and wheelchairs. Fresh-faced doctors clutch manila folders as they mispronounce foreign names.

"Mrs Zablinsky," a doctor calls. No one stands. The name is called again.

"Do you mean Mrs Zwabbley?"

The doctor checks his file and nods.

Strangers strike friendly conversations, babies cry, mobile phones seem to be ever ringing. One energetic toddler toddles off at a fast pace, closely followed by his mother.

"Got you," his mother said, grabbing at the child. The toddler in defiance plonks himself on the floor.

"Come on; I'm in no mood for races today." She carries the protesting child back to her seat.

There is a steady *thump*, *thump* of patients and medical staff marching back and forth on the echoing corridor. A flotteria of men with similar black suits appear to flow past. Behind, in their slipstream, are younger doctors, almost skipping trying to catch up, with stethoscopes dangling around their necks.

Paula has her head in her book, *Madam Bovary*. Rachael interacts with the games on her mobile phone.

"Mum, I need to pee," Rachel said in a loud agitated voice.

Several people turn to look.

Here we go again.

Paula's face reddens.

They drape their coats over the back of the seats, a soft option to maintain ownership of their seats. Rachael's crutches clank as they trudge to the toilet.

"Oh no, I wet myself," Rachael cries from inside the toilet.

"No matter, I have a change of clothes." Paula's voice is resigned. She passes the clean tracksuit pants and underpants under the door, exchanges the wet ones. Opens a plastic bag from the handbag and pops the wet clothes in the bag.

"I hate this," Rachel wails from the cubicle.

"It will get better with time."

They return to the waiting room to find two elder European men sitting in their seats.

"Excuse me, these are our seats," Paula said with a forced smile.

The men shake their heads. "No comprendo."

Paula tries to yank the black coat from under one man.

"Get off our fucking coats!" screams Rachael.

"Bastardo," said one. He makes a rude gesture with a finger. The men move to the back, spill against the wall.

"They stole our seats, and they tried to steal our coats." Rachael's voice is louder and louder. Heads turn towards them.

"Please be quiet Rachael," Tears of rage spring up in Paula's eyes. She wants to vanish.

Rachael empties her pockets and finds a half-eaten Mars bar. She stares at Paula as she chomps with her mouth open, displaying chocolate saliva.

"Close your mouth when you chew."

"Yar...yar..." Rachel slides a hand over her mouth, wipes the sticky goo over the tracksuit.

Paula studies her watch.

Why does she have to be like this? It is so embarrassing.

"Why are we here?" asks Rachael.

"To have a review with the doctor."

"What's he going to do?" asks Rachael.

"Check on your progress."

Rachael asks, "Why are we here? How long do we have to wait?" at least ten times.

"However long it takes."

When the doctor sees them, he is full of praise. "Rachael, you're doing so well."

Paula bites her tongue so hard she can taste blood.

THIRTEEN

Life moves on
May 2003, Kensington

THREE DAYS A WEEK, A SIX-SEATER WHITE VAN DRIVES up Westbourne Road and toots its horn. A door slams and Rachael shambles to the van.

"Hi, guys."

"Did you bring your bathers?" asks a blonde girl.

Rachael holds up a bag.

The teenagers have a busy day scheduled at the outpatient rehabilitation centre. First on the list is physiotherapy in the heated pool. Then a break for lunch, followed by occupational therapy. They plan to cook date scones for afternoon tea. Teachers will mark homework and assign work based on individual capabilities.

Alone at last, Colin pours a second cup of coffee, finishes reading the paper before starting work.

The garage has wall-to-wall shelving, crammed to overflowing with tools and gadgets. A few years ago, he installed black drapes. When they're drawn, it resembles a room. They open to expose tools and working areas. The wide wooden workbench is made to specifications. The bench width reaches both sides of the wall and has multiple drawers on either side.

This is my personal space.

He shrugs his shoulders and recalls Paula's attempts at neatening the garage.

"What are you doing?" he had asked.

"Tidying up the mess..."

"Everything is in order." His face is dark. "Ask permission before you touch anything."

~

Colin buys and sells specialized engineering and train stock via the internet. His website, Colin's Engineering, Train and Constructions, has hundreds of hits daily by the international and local liked-minded community. A variety of large, wooden boxes marked "Engineering Equipment" is delivered by express courier to the garage. Colin repairs what he can. The larger pieces of stock are stored at Newport yards. Colin has a contract with the management, assists steam rail to service the trains, and has the option to use their storage facilities.

Colin is shrewd with money, makes a good profit from the business. He perfected an eye for buying vital pieces. Railway companies interact with him; he is known as a hard-nosed but fair operator. The garage is the heartbeat of his life, he spends days challenged by mechanical issues, is stoked when he solves complex problems. He keeps up with world news and snippets of local events from the radio between the whir of machines.

Paula is content to return to full-time teaching, relieved to have space from the unfixable issues at home.

I haven't got a minute to spare.

Paula is a second-year coordinator for social work students and maintains a gruelling teaching and tutorial role. Preparations for the next day's teaching take place after Rachael's dramas are sorted and the evening meal finishes, and dishes washed.

Paula's areas of research are diverse. Homelessness and food distribution, compliance of outpatient appointments after suicide attempts and, her favourite, post-traumatic stress outcomes for survivors of torture. She is a recognised expert in these fields and a popular speaker at conferences. She is active in university committees and a staunch advocate for student rights.

"Paula is amazing, so switched on," one student remarks.

"She is arrogant," comments a colleague to another.

"I am worried about Paula," Jenny said to friend Adriana over coffee.

"She should slow down, she pushes herself too hard."

"I guess she is compensating for things she can't control," said Adriana.

Work colleagues are supportive. Even the grumpy Head of School showed guarded concern for a while and then reverted to his old self.

"I want you to chair the research committee meeting on Friday." He hands Paula a pile of student proposals and funding applications to be scrutinized before the meeting.

Any colleagues foolish enough to inquire as to Rachael's current progress receive the stock standard answer.

"Rachael's body is mended."

Paula is annoyed by their probing. Her home life is off limits. If anyone persists in asking invasive questions, she changes the conversation. She hates that they gossip about her family. She never mentions Rachael's neurological problems.

Sarah is either at school, library, or her room. She generally has her nose in a textbook or crouched over the computer. Her bedroom door closed to the raised voices and irritable shouting that is part of Rachael's chaos. Sarah calculated that Cambridge is twenty-four hours away from Melbourne by plane and plans to achieve the best results possible—win a scholarship. Her dream is to study Anthropology at Cambridge.

"Why Cambridge?" asks Colin. "There are good universities here in Australia."

"Cambridge has the best Anthropology course

in the world." She wasn't sure, but it sounds possible.

Colin is proud of both his daughters. But has great expectations for Sarah.

❧

When Sarah was born, Colin carried her to the window and pointed out the lights of the city.

"This is Melbourne city."

He touched the softness of minuscule fingers. An ache formed somewhere deep.

I will be a good father, not like my father.

❧

Colin's father Harold had terrorized his wife Eleanor, who ballooned into an obese woman. She spent her life cleaning, cooking, and watching television. Eleanor used to scurry to the kitchen as soon as she heard his car drive up and made a show of banging saucepans to show she had been preparing the evening meal.

Harold tried to control his three sons, but they learned his combative skills and stood up for each other. If he berated one son, the other brother came to his aide.

"It was me that did it, Dad," they said in unison.

"We kicked the football that broke the window," they said.

The three agreed to leave home as soon as they

finished secondary school. Colin, at eighteen, moved to a cheap flat to join the older brothers to study engineering.

Harold died of a heart attack at sixty-four. Eleanor collected the life insurance, paid out the mortgage, and joined the local Elderly Citizen Club. She looked forward to bus trips to Bright and Anglesea. On a whim, she attended Weight Watchers and slimmed to a voluptuous size sixteen. A man at the club took an interest in her and wanted to marry. Eleanor refused his proposal but allowed him to stay overnight twice a week.

Colin and his brothers, Max and Gerald, stayed close. They met up at the for the football and Friday night bistro at the Waterloo Hotel until Gerard died from prostate cancer, leaving a wife and a secret girlfriend.

~

A sister of a friend introduced Colin to Paula. He thought Paula was a beautiful creature from another planet. Colin pursued her for months until she agreed to go out with him.

Eleanor liked Paula. "Hang on to this one, she's special."

They married when Paula finished her degree. Eleanor died eight months after the wedding.

~

"You are so beautiful." Colin had kissed baby Sarah tenderly on her forehead. "I wish my mother was alive. She would have loved you," he said.

FOURTEEN

The bones heal
June 2003

THE METAL PIN HAS BEEN REMOVED FROM RACHEL'S leg, the bone healed. The main frustration is her poor memory and fear of losing things.

"Did you touch my book? I can't find it," she asked.

She still has word-finding difficulty and speaks in a husky, hesitant voice. Rachael's hair has grown back to its normal light brown colour and thick texture.

Colin runs his hands over the softness and calls her *fluffy duck*.

The accident trapped Rachael in a younger brain than her years. She has the blossoming body of an adolescent with messy periods, swelling breasts, mood swings, and acne. The injury affected the executive area of the frontal lobe. She cannot understand abstract concepts and takes words on face value.

"Did you have a fine day?" brings the response, "It wasn't fine yesterday; it rained."

She suffers nightmares and sleeps with the

light on. Is impulsive, demanding, has little understanding of others' feelings. Her only friends are those from the rehabilitation group. Rachael spends time alone watching *Gilligan's Island* and *MASH* repeats, smokes cigarettes in secret in the garden shed.

Colin jokes and pulls funny faces to make her laugh.

"Dad, you're dill," she said.

The tortoise, Doris, wanders around the garden. He's never in the handsome hutch made with wire and wood, is found by the gate, near the garage, at the back doorstep, often sleeping in the rose garden.

"Watch out; don't step on Doris," is a regular call.

Every week, Rachael places the tortoise in a plastic bucket with warm water, scrubs the withered old shell with an old toothbrush. He pulls his neck and legs inside the shell creating a lock. She oils and polishes the shell until it shines.

The other Doris is thriving in the new nursing home. She uses every chance to attack Paula.

"If you were a decent daughter, you'd stop working and look after me properly."

Colin refuses to visit.

FIFTEEN

The bag
June 2003

IT TAKES CAREFUL PLANNING FOR PAULA TO LEAVE THE house for work. She rises at the usual time, 5:30, showers, and dresses in clothes chosen the day before. Most days she wears beige or black slacks, adding a coloured shirt and black jacket. When she wears a skirt, it's either plain black or grey.

For the past ten years, Paula has hovered around a size eight to ten, weighs 54kg. Each morning, naked, jumps on the scales, frowns if the scale goes up even a fraction, and vows to put in another aerobic session. Paula's fair hair is mid-shoulder length; she keeps it to a classic bob. She always eats one piece of toast and black tea for breakfast.

Colin is fixated on a daily routine of four crushed Weetabix, cold milk, chopped up banana, and yogurt. His breakfast plans include not being disturbed while eating breakfast and spreading *The Age* out on the table.

"I'm teaching the post-grads tonight; I will be home after nine. There is a chicken casserole and rice in the fridge. Fruit for dessert," she said.

He looks up, "Write a note. You know I forget."

"What are your plans for today?" she said.

He looks up from the paper. "Donald Engineering is having a fire sale. I might poke around and see if there's anything I could use."

"Make sure Rachael is awake at 7:30." She kisses him on the cheek. "Don't forget to ring Max for his birthday," she said.

He looks as though hearing her for the first time.

Her briefcase holds reports, lecture notes, SD card, and committee meetings briefings. She developed her own *to do list*, which maps each hour from 0500 until midnight. One side marked for important tasks and the other section for comments.

"Don't be late tonight," he always says that.

"I'll try," she usually responds.

≈

Colin pursued Paula for weeks until she agreed to go out with him. He talked. She listened. He assumed she liked him and cared as he did. Paula never experienced the giddy in-love feelings of other girls. Colin was dependable, and more importantly, a chance to escape from home.

They married in a registry office with the small circle of family and friends, celebrated at a local Italian restaurant. At first, they rented a small flat.

Over time, it made way for an old house in Ascot Vale and the move to Kensington where they live now.

When Colin's mother died, the brothers sold the family home and split the money between them. The Wilson family bought a tiny beach house at Indented Head. Every free weekend and holidays, they loaded the car and escaped to the beach.

~

Paula was uncertain how to mother her own children. She read child-rearing books, swallowed the latest theories related to child bonding and intelligence. She scrutinized friends for tips on how to have a happy life. Children's birthday parties, celebrations, and play dates were learned by watching other women, other mothers. Paula had an unwavering resolve to be a proper mother.

Sarah and Rachael had a dress-up box of miscellaneous clothes collected from charity shops. It contained a stained wedding dress, a flight attendant's uniform, and half a nurse's outfit. There was an assortment of hats, scarves, shawls, bags, and shoes. The girls draped sheets across chairs, fashioned extravagant dramas with musical themes. Colin and Paula were special guests, and they applauded with pleasure and loud bravos.

It was only when Sarah and Rachael attended the local primary school that Paula returned to study, completing a master's degree in Social Work, then a PhD. Her self-esteem grew. She landed a sought-after job as an academic. Students listened, and colleagues respected her. She recreated, restructured her identity, and became someone.

SIXTEEN

The cold chill that wakes
November 2003, Kensington

PAULA WOKE UP FROM A DEEP SLEEP WITH A FEELING of foreboding, of danger and a chill in her heart. She pulled on her dressing gown and went downstairs.

She remembered Aunt Bertha telling her, "When someone experiences a cold chill that wakes them from sleep, it means the dead are floating nearby. They are trying to warn of impending doom."

Aunt Bertha told a story of waking up with the chill, hearing her dead father call out.

"Don't take the number 465 to town today."

Aunt Bertha heeded his advice and walked to work. The bus crashed, two killed and eleven injured.

~

Paula shivers, wraps the dressing gown tight. *What I need is a hot cup of tea.*

~

Her father Stan would not be capable of warning of impending doom. Doris had ordered every detail of their lives. He rarely did anything on his own.

Things changed when Stan developed dementia; he discovered inner rebellion and strength.

"You're not the boss of me," he shouted at Doris.

Her mouth opened, threatened all manner of possible harms. Stan ignored her. With his head held high, he stomped to the bedroom and slammed the door.

One day, Stan fell, fracturing a hip. A traveling blood clot ended up in a lung and he died. Doris changed overnight from a demanding harridan to a fearful woman who always needed company.

Paula couldn't understand Doris's newfound helplessness. Her mother became afraid to stay in the small flat, hearing too many noises and fearful creaking. Became reliant on others to cook and clean.

"I'm on the scrap heap of life," Doris said, dabbing her eyes with a floral handkerchief.

Paula bit her nails.

She organized a gentle, live-in lady to help Doris. But she did not stay long, citing Doris's endless complaints.

"Good riddance," said Doris. "The sink was never cleaned properly. The towels not folded the right way." A smug expression plastered over her face.

Paula organised Meals on Wheels. After a week,

they stopped delivering the meals to Doris as she declared their food only fit for pigs.

The district nurse calculated Doris's morning shower was equivalent, in time, to showering three other patients. That included traveling and the keeping of logbooks.

Her complaints are driving me crazy.

Paula turned pale when Doris's phone number came up on her mobile. She often muted the phone for hours.

The agency sent a Division two nurse, at double cost, to attend to Doris. She lasted the morning.

"You can't be a real nurse as you're too fat," Doris had told her.

"I quit. Your mother is the rudest person I have ever met," said the nurse.

There's no pleasing my mother, thought Paula.

Paula developed an appetite for potato crisps, as soon as one bag was emptied, she searched for another.

When other avenues of care were exhausted, a jubilant Doris moved into Paula and Colin's home.

"I want the larger bedroom," Doris said with arms folded.

"Our room is not available." Paula imagined Colin's outcry if he had to move to the spare room.

Paula shrugged her shoulders and opened another bag of potato crisps.

Colin entertained fantasies of tying Doris to a chair and sailing her down the Maribyrnong River.

Rachael and Sarah avoided Doris, disappearing to friends' homes or disappeared into their rooms to do homework.

Doris hated to be left in the house during the day when everyone was at work or school. The minute Paula arrives home it starts.

"I'm alone here. You must stop working and look after me properly."

Not in your life will I stay at home and look after you, thought Paula.

Doris refused to attend any clubs, "Too many old people." She rejected the local church group, which provided a small bus for outings.

Paula developed a nervous tic and repeatedly blinked.

"It would be polite to allow me to watch the Channel Seven news, instead of the ABC news. And I prefer the *Herald Sun* delivered; I hate *The Age* newspaper," she said to Colin.

Colin turned the sound up on the TV.

"Either Doris goes into a nursing home or I leave." Colin made an elaborate show of packing a suitcase and rang his brother Max.

"If you're going, I'm coming with you," said Rachael.

"Me too," said Sarah.

Paula clenched her fists, made a list of the local aged care homes. But, it was Rachael's accident that forced Doris into care. Paula had neither the time nor energy for Doris's relentless demands.

Despite the trauma of the accident, Paula ceased nibbling on her nails. The appetite for potato crisps evaporated.

~

Tonight, Paula is in the kitchen warming her hands around the hot mug. Then restless, she wanders through the house. She peers into Sarah's room, she is asleep.

Paula notices strange noises from Rachael's room, opens the door, Rachael is swirling in circles, hair flying and babbling in a strange language. It is as though Sarah is moving in time to unseen music.

"Rachael?"

"Humpty Dumpty sat on the wall. Humpty Dumpty had a great fall," said Rachael.

"Rachael?"

"And all the kings' horses and all the kings' men could never fix Humpty Dumpty again." She stares at Paula. "If I stop twirling, I'll be shot."

Paula runs to Colin. He tries to restrain Rachael; eventually they bundle Rachael into the car, Paula holding her arms as he drives.

"I'll be shot," Rachael screams.

At the hospital they are told by a young doctor, "Rachael is having a psychotic episode. The on-call psychiatrist will confirm the diagnosis."

Paula and Colin slump on the chairs. An

hour passes, then another. Eventually, they are summoned by an older doctor.

"I am Dr Hamilton, the psychiatrist attending Rachael. The good news is that Rachael is not having a psychotic episode." He fiddles with his pen.

"It appears that Rachael has taken the drug ecstasy." He pauses.

"Tests confirm it. The ecstasy has reacted with the seizure medication Rachael takes," he said.

"Every so often the party drugs get out of hand. Rachael told us she has been experimenting with a number of drugs for a while." He watches their faces.

He puts a hand on Paula's shoulder.

"Rachael will be all right. We have given her medication to reduce the effect. I think she should stay here overnight, so we can observe her. If all goes well, you can pick her up tomorrow."

Paula puts her hand to her chest. She can hardly breathe.

Oh my God, how am I supposed to cope with drug taking; when is it ever going to end?

Colin is speechless.

SEVENTEEN

The DVD player
July 2004

PAULA STANDS AT THE WINDOW OF HER OFFICE AT THE University; she watches a group of students taking advantage of the meek sunshine. They huddle under trees and squat on the grass. A brass band plays somewhere in the distance.

Rachael has been too quiet these days. No dramatic outbursts, no screaming.

When Paula returns home, she notices an empty space in the lounge room shelf where the DVD player normally sits.

"Is our DVD player broken?" She said to Colin.

"Not that I know."

"It's missing from its spot," she said.

"Perhaps someone stole it," he said.

"Why would anyone steal the DVD player and nothing else?"

"Maybe the girls took it to watch in their rooms," he said, distracted. He holds a piece of metal that had a small hole in the middle.

Paula finds Rachael sprawled on her bed,

headphones clamped over ears, heavy metal music leaking out from the headphones.

"Did you take the DVD player?" Paula shouts, lifting the headphones from Rachael's ear.

"You weren't using it," Rachael said, pulling the earphones back.

"Why?"

"I needed the money. You don't give me a proper allowance." Glares at Paula.

"Rachael, you are paid for jobs to be done around the home. No jobs, no allowance." Paula stands with her hands crossed.

"Why do you need money? If it was important you could have asked me."

"The DVD player is at Cash Converters. I owed a friend money," Rachael shrugs her shoulders.

"What...?" Paula is momentarily shocked.

"You stole our property to repay a debt. This is bizarre," Paula's cheeks redden.

"Don't make such a big deal out of it. My friend needed the money straight away. I had no money, so I took the player. I'll get it back when I receive my next allowance."

Rachael has a trace of a smile, watches the red blush spread down Paula's neck.

"Here's the ticket." She throws the receipt on the bed.

"Anyway, no one uses a DVD player; they play movies on computers. You haven't used the player in months."

"That's not the point." Impotent fury flares out from Paula.

Rachael clamps the headphones over her ears and returns to the magazine.

Paula has dark suspicions but is unable to say anything. Her throat tightens. She drives to Cash Converters, buys back the player, places it back in the lounge.

EIGHTEEN

Max's wife Barbara
August 2004

BARBARA HATES HOUSEWORK; THE HOUSE IS shambolic. Unfolded clothes from the clothesline pile on the lounge. The breakfast dishes wait to be washed. Unopened bills are strewn on the bench.

Barbara falls on the sofa, lets out a sigh.

"I am so tired of running around for everyone," she said.

"But Mum," said a male voice. He bounces a basketball in one hand. "I really want pizza now."

"Sorry, Trevor, there's no chance of my going out again. If you're hungry, make a sandwich."

He slams the back door, the ball crunches on the cement and clanks against the wire net.

Kids think you're a machine, Barbara thought.

The door bangs open again.

"Mum?" the ball spinning on his finger.

"I saw Sarah today. Why is she so skinny?" He makes a face pulling in his cheeks.

"I haven't seen Sarah for a while, perhaps she's sick. Why don't you go over to Sarah's and say hello? Perhaps she needs a friend." she said.

"I hate going to Sarah's house; it gives me the creeps. Everything is so damn neat. I never know where to sit," he said.

"Not like our messy place." She laughs. Gets up and stacks the dishes to one side and runs the hot water in the sink.

He opens the cupboard. "Yeah…food."

He pulls a pack of potato crisps from the back and disappears. Loud music floods the house.

"Turn down the volume," she shouts.

He slams the bedroom door.

～

Last month, Barbara ran into Paula at the local shopping centre.

"We're having a party next Saturday to celebrate Max's promotion. Why don't you all join us? It will be fun."

Paula hesitated. "I think we have something on that Saturday."

The last thing Paula wants is to spend the evening at Barbara and Max's home. To be encompassed in thick tobacco smoke, barking dogs, children running amok, and noisy, inebriated adults.

"I'm going to bingo tonight. Do you want me to pick you up and we could go together?" Barbara added.

"Mmm, I have a few papers to mark tonight," Paula trails.

"Another time then…" Barbara said.

NINETEEN

Life changes in an instant
March 2005

"Time to wake up, Rachel," said Paula sticking her head in the room. "You will be late."

No reply.

She enters Rachael's room and bends over the sleeping girl. She speaks loudly in her ear.

"Time to wake up," again no response. "Rachael, can you hear me?"

Paula shakes Rachael. No movement. Paula's voice increases in volume, almost screaming.

"Rachael, wake up!"

She checks her daughter's pulse.

I can't feel a pulse, is she dead? Her face looks bluish...

Her heart beats like a runaway stallion; she runs to the bathroom, wets a face cloth and rubs the soaking cloth over Rachael's face. Again, no response from Rachael.

"For God's sake, wake up!"

Paula shakes her vigorously. Nothing...

"Colin," Paula shouts on the top of her lungs.

"Come quickly, something has happened to Rachael."

Colin rushes in, followed by Sarah.

"What's going on?" says Colin. "You scared me..." He stands in his pyjamas.

Sarah is wild-eyed, mouth open.

"I can't wake Rachael. I am not sure if she's alive or dead."

"Is she sick?" He said.

Paula shakes her head.

"Sarah, call triple 000, ask for the ambulance. Tell them Rachael is not able to be aroused. I'm not sure if she's breathing. Tell them I can't feel a pulse." Paula sweats. Her veins pulsate in her neck.

"Make sure you give them our address."

Sarah runs to find her mobile.

It's always something with Rachael.

Paula and Colin roll Rachael onto her back and commence mouth-to-mouth resuscitation. They count and breathe and count and push on her chest. Rachael's body stays limp. Rachael's lips blue, hands and legs are floppy.

They look at each other with terror in their eyes.

"The ambulance is on its way. It'll be here in ten minutes," Sarah comes in breathless.

Paula runs her fingers over Rachael's eyelashes, there is no flickering.

She turns to Sarah. "Where's the damn ambulance? Go downstairs and wait for them."

Colin's gut churns, he wants to vomit but continues with the resuscitation.

Several minutes later, two paramedics run up the stairs followed by Sarah.

They assess the situation, shine a torch into Rachael's eyes, and undertake a variety of tests. Then inject Narcan and, within seconds, colour comes back to Rachael's face and she stirs.

"Heroin overdose," said the female officer.

"Lucky you found her when you did. A few minutes more and she might have died."

Paula tugs at her fingers.

What does she mean? Did my daughter use heroin in my home?

Colin cracks his knuckles, clenches his hands. Wants to hurt something, gives a guttural roar.

"Heroin. Are you sure?"

"We can deal with this, keep calm," said Paula.

Sarah has a glassy expression on her face and covers her ears.

I gave her the money. She said she wanted to buy a pair of jeans.

"No need to take her to the hospital unless she slips into a coma again," said the paramedic.

"Here is a hint: I have been to a number of heroin overdoses." She stares into their faces. "Be prepared for your daughter's anger; you will get no thanks for saving her life. She'll be furious about the heroin wasted. The Narcan will have nullified the effect of the heroin."

Alarm spreads over the faces of Paula and Colin.

"Try not to be caught up in her anger."

The paramedic scrawls a report and leaves.

Paula and Colin cannot speak. Sarah sobs.

A sound comes from the bed.

"What are you all doing crowding in my room?" Rachael's voice sounds unfamiliar, strange, filled with contempt.

"Does anyone want a cup of tea?" asked Colin through clenched teeth, a murderous look on his face.

"I'll help," said Sarah.

"Why did you call the ambulance?" Rachael glares at Paula.

"You wasted $100 of heroin." Rachael's face is hard and defiant.

"I hate you."

"How long have you been using heroin?" said Paula. Her voice careful, controlled.

After all we have done for her. How could she do this to our family?

Rachael ignores the question, fiddles with her hair.

Paula smells Nag Champa incense stick burning on the window ledge. It fills the room, dead and offensive. Paula throws the essence stick in the bin, it clangs.

Rachael raises an eyebrow, says nothing.

Here it comes.... Mother will go on and on about

the evils of heroin. What would she know? The only knowledge she has is what she has read from textbooks.

Excited dogs bark outside. A motor mower starts in the street. An alien drug world has crashed into the street and entered their home.

Rachael runs her fingers through her hair.

"Why is my hair wet?"

Paula ignores the question.

"How long have you been using?" asked Paula again, her voice is slow and deliberate. She leans into Rachael's face, Rachael pulls back.

"None of your damn business…"

Rachael avoids her mother's gaze.

They square off at each other.

Hate pouring out of Rachael.

Fury from Paula.

Colin comes in with a tray of steaming cups of tea. He passes a cup to Paula, offers a cup to Rachael; she ignores him and turns her body away from him facing the wall.

"We're decent people, we don't produce drug addicts. How could you do this, to your family?" Colin said.

Sarah is silent, the colour drained from her face.

How was I to know she wanted the money for heroin? It would have been my fault if she died.

"How long, Rachael?" Paula persists.

"Long enough…"

"You almost died today," Paula said.

"It's my life."

"We don't deserve this," said Colin.

"Thanks for nothing." Rachael twists the sheet avoiding their gaze.

"You're going into drug treatment," Paula said.

"I'm not going anywhere." Rachael crosses her arms.

They don't even want to understand why I used. They have no idea.

"While you live under this roof, you will obey the rules. This is a drug-free home. The recreational use of ecstasy was one thing. Heroin is another story altogether." Paula said.

Colin nods in agreement.

"I am warning you, we will pull this room apart to check if you have any more drugs hidden somewhere. And…we will do regular spot checks." Paula's voice is distant as though reading a script, a learned response.

Sarah leaves the room, unwilling to be involved, to even listen to the madness.

TWENTY

The perfect cover
June 2005

THERE ARE NO BOUNDARIES WITH HEROIN; IT infiltrates the lives of those around the user. Paula and Colin attempted to remove every vestige of heroin and drug paraphernalia from Rachael's room. They found bent, burnt spoons, used syringes jammed behind the dressing table. They emptied every cupboard, drawer. Shoes were tipped out, jeans, hoodies, jackets, tops emptied of worn tissues and rubbish.

Rachael watches them with a bemused expression and smirks at a private joke.

It is delicious to see Mother so inflamed and out of control. They think they are so clever. They will never find my secret stash.

"Do you think I would be stupid enough to hide it here?" Rachael said.

Paula catches Rachael's furtive glance towards a toy sitting on the window sill. She grabs the soft penguin. She runs her fingers along the seam and locates a small plastic pouch containing white powder.

"Colin..." she said.

Rachael looks away.

Colin handles the pouch with two fingers as though it's a bomb.

He shakes his head.

"I don't know what to say."

Paula closes her eyes, tries to stop the momentum of panic. The line is blurred between safe home and the outside world.

Rachael stands with her arms hanging by her side.

They took my stash. I will be sick...

Sometime later Rachael goes into withdrawals. Paula is there during the sweating, the throwing up, the diarrhoea, and the soiled bed drenched in sweat. Days later, Rachael improves, confidence blooming. She appears to have turned the corner. But her drug dealer waits. He knows it will be a matter of time before she will search for him.

Pandemonium is the new normal in the household. Trust disappears, replaced with paranoia and suspicion and unending anger.

～

Heroin had become the putty that filled the cracks in Rachael's life. It became an oasis and the best part of the day. With it, she could function. But without the heroin, she was disturbed and restless.

She still uses heroin whenever she can, despite the surveillance and weekly urine tests.

Everything is about the next hit.

Rachael is adept at stealing small amounts of money and valuables from the family to pay for her drug habit.

Paula can't shake the guilt and shame. She feels like a failure as a mother, searches the internet, jots notes related to programs, rings Direct line for advice, inquiries into youth substance abuse services, detoxification, and rehabilitation. Paula drags Rachael to numerous treatment appointments.

Rachael, at sixteen, is a match for Paula. She has no intention of stopping. Not yet. She stumbled on a magic elixir which makes life bearable, no way is going to stop.

"Why do you use?" Paula asks over and over as if trying to understand.

"Because I love it."

Heroin is pure pleasure. Why can't they understand?

These days, Paula seems to have a face set in a hard edge. She snaps at students, is impatient with colleagues. She argues at meetings over inconsequential points. Colleagues keep a wide berth. Students stop popping into her office to ask questions.

The atmosphere at home is toxic. Colin and Paula snap at each other. They can barely acknowledge Rachael. Regardless, Rachael's pupils are often pinned and her speech slow and slurred.

Sarah has learned the art of being invisible in a house of chaos.

Drug counselling does not help. They try the Suboxone program. Rachael became bored with the daily pharmacy visits.

She is oblivious to the heroin's effect on the family. They are all on a drug merry-go-round. Up and down, up and down. When the music of the drug use starts, they respond. When the music of the drug use stops, all are affected by Rachael's withdrawals.

The fights at home escalate, become poisonous. Paula arranges for Rachael to go to a Narcotics Anonymous meeting and waits in the car. For a few weeks, it works. The family gives a collective sigh of relief. But they learn Rachael has been slipping away during the meetings and scoring with another NA member.

Rachael is drug-free for four weeks after a detox. Then she met an old friend who offered a taste, which became a full relapse.

"Let's try detox again," said Paula. "It takes a while for a new behaviour to stick."

Paula's hair shows evidence of grey, a permanent frown decked on her face.

Colin is always furious, impotent of any power in his own home.

"You're killing yourself with that stuff," he said, his voice booming louder than usual.

His arms are always crossed when he speaks to Rachael, as though protecting himself from her. He cannot separate the drug heroin from the person who is his daughter. In his mind, Rachael has morphed into heroin. He is out of his depth. Rachael's drug use violates a hidden part of Colin; he bristles with righteous anger. The shouting and abuse escalate to the point where he shoves her out of the front door.

"I didn't plan to get hooked," said Rachael to Colin. Her hands tremble, she blinks.

"I hate this more than you do."

"You haven't tried hard enough." Colin spits the words out.

Now and then, household things vanish. Paula buys them back from Cash Converters.

Colin invests in a steel safe in the bedroom, bolts the safe to the floor. They keep valuables, cheque books, and credit cards in the safe. He installs a thick padlock and elaborate locking system to protect his tools in his garage.

Paula carries her red purse inside her bra.

The local police come to the house. Rachael shoplifts from stores. She is caught on CTTV cameras.

Sarah loathes the fights. Her parents scream at Rachael and at each other or don't speak for days.

Sarah lives as a boarder, makes no demands. and stays with her friend Tracey.

On Wednesday, Colin and Rachael engage in another bitter argument when he discovers $200 taken from his wallet while he was in the shower.

"You stole it." He points at Rachael.

"I never thought I'd live to see the day when my own daughter stoops so low."

"I need to get the gear," she whispers, there are beads of perspiration on her upper lip.

"Get out." He pushes her down the steps.

"I live here," Rachael's voice childlike.

She bangs on the door and then creeps away.

Later, when it is dark, Paula pulls on the old black coat and searches for Rachael. By now she is familiar with the dark alleyways, the hidden areas; the McDonald's where addicts crouch together. She drags a reluctant Rachael home, dishevelled and dirty. Feeds her, puts her to bed.

"I'm teaching Rachael tough love. You ruin it bringing her home," Colin's voice like thunder. He blames Paula.

"She's sixteen. It's not safe at night."

Colin spends increasing time with Max at the pub. Rants and raves, makes rude comments aimed at a young man with tattoos sitting at the bar.

"I should go over and punch him; he looks like a drug dealer." He grimaces.

"I should get a gun and shoot the dog that's supplying drugs to Rachael."

Paula finds bloodied tissues in Sarah's rubbish bin. "Are you bleeding?"

"Shaved my legs," said Sarah.

When driving to work, she remembers Sarah waxes her legs. By the time she returns home, it is forgotten and Rachael's latest drama envelopes the family.

Sarah is often in the school library.

"Is everything okay?" Mrs Gilbert said noticing Sarah's forlorn expression.

"No problems." she said. Her voice registers resignation.

Sarah stops.

"Mrs Gilbert, is it hard to obtain an overseas scholarship? I want to study anthropology at Cambridge."

Mrs Gilbert understood.

"A great idea. Come and see me at lunch time."

They develop a study plan that will enhance Sarah's scholarship chances. The Anthropology degree soon develops a life of its own. It has become a secret code that signals escape.

Mrs Gilbert uncovers books on anthropology, advises study schedules.

Together they submit the Cambridge scholarship application.

TWENTY-ONE

Borrowing money
June 2005

"IT'S BEEN AGES SINCE WE HAD COFFEE," JENNY LEANS towards Paula.

They are at the Boathouse restaurant near the river. Rowers in bright colours glide past on the water. Mothers scurry past with babies in prams dragging unenthusiastic dogs on leashes.

"You look terrible; what's going on?" asked Jenny, spreading the napkin over her knees.

Paula is silent for a while, and whispers, "Rachael is injecting heroin."

Jenny bites her lip.

"Oh, my goodness," she said.

Paula proceeds to inform Jenny about Rachael and the heroin overdose. How they search the house daily for drugs, how she refuses treatment. She tells about the inordinate time and effort to try to stop her using heroin.

"How horrible for you, it must be a nightmare. How is Colin coping?"

"Colin blames me for the situation. He is determined to deal with Rachael with tough love, throwing her out of the house if she uses. But she is only a child. She is so vulnerable. The situation is tearing us apart. We argue all the time. It's terrible."

Her eyes brim with tears, looks at her nails.

"This is much worse than the head injury. This is much worse." She looks up.

"I was ashamed to tell you. Afraid you would judge me as a rotten mother."

"You're a wonderful mother. Stop beating up on yourself." Jenny holds Paula's hand.

"No one knows how to deal with their kids on drugs. What works for one does not work for another. It sounds as though you are doing your best. These kids are smart. Rachael is one step ahead of you."

"Why didn't you speak to me earlier? I could have helped with resources." Jenny said.

"You won't like what I am about to say." Jenny sucks in her bottom lip.

"I was going to tell you, when the time was right."

"Rachael came to my house and wanted $100. She had a lame excuse that she wanted to buy you a surprise present."

"Did you give her money?" Paula places her hand over her mouth.

"I had $50. Rachael took that. She was acting a little weird, staring at my handbag."

Jenny signals to the waitress for more coffee.

"Rachael asked Adriana for money, but she

never carries cash. Rachael suggested they go to the ATM. But Adriana refused."

Paula covers her face.

"Oh no. Not Adriana. I can't bear—"

"Stop it, Paula. No one's judging you."

Paula flinches.

They stare out of the window.

"How is Sarah in all of this?" asks Jenny.

"Sarah has become a hermit, hiding from the family. Staying with friends" says Paula.

"Rachael has always been the family's favourite." Jenny holds a hand up.

"No, don't argue. Anyone can see that the family functions for Rachael."

Paula opens her mouth to speak but no words come out.

"I've worked for years with problem adolescents. The quiet ones also suffer."

Jenny glances at Paula who is holding her head in her hands. She pulls Paula's hand away from her face.

"It sounds as though you are doing what you can with Rachael. Hopefully, she will grow out of it. Most kids do. They experiment for a while and then move on to other things like boyfriends."

Paula fidgets, is visibly annoyed, looks away.

"No time for guilt. You did what you could. I want to give Sarah special attention," said Jenny.

She smiles at a small child who toddles past their table.

Paula blows her nose.

"I was going to surprise you, invite you on a short break to Brampton Island. I won a week for two in a competition," says Jenny.

"Sarah could come with me."

"Why Sarah? Rachael could use a holiday."

"The last thing I need is Rachael acting up or withdrawing on the trip."

She shakes her head.

"No, Sarah needs a break more."

Paula's face is ashen. Her voice shakes.

"I think Sarah may be self-harming," she said.

TWENTY-TWO

Brampton Island
June 2005

Brampton Island greets Sarah and Jenny in lazy splendour. The temperature burning hot, the clear beach goes for miles. They book in the hotel, dump their bags on the bed, change into beach gear and check out the island.

Sarah skips with pleasure.

Jenny grins.

The tide is out, disappeared somewhere in the horizon. Jenny maintains a spot on a cane lounge under a palm tree. Carefully soothes suntan lotion over her body and sighs.

"Ahh, perfect."

Sarah explores the island.

"Hey," said Sarah, flopping next to Jenny.

"So glad you won the prize and allowed me to come with you." She beams.

"Would you believe the owners have a pet emu, strolls around as if he owns the place? See that tiny island?" She points in the distance.

"There's a boat stuck in the sand."

A silver-haired couple walk past, arm in arm.

Jenny sits up. "Come and sit next to me. I have a few things to discuss." She pats the lounge seat next to her.

"Do we have to?" Sarah rolls her eyes, dreading what is to follow.

Even here the world revolves around Rachael.

"Your mother spoke to me about what is going on with Rachael."

Sarah groans. "It's always about Rachael."

"And...Paula mentioned you were having issues, too."

Sarah shields her face from the sun.

"What did she say about me?" Frowns.

"I have worked hard at staying out of the daily Rachael dramas."

Jenny nods. "Rachael does suck the oxygen out of your family." Speaks slowly trying not to frighten Sarah, lowers her voice.

"I never told anyone before, but when I was younger I used to cut myself."

Sarah makes a face and is about to get up. Jenny grabs her arm.

"Wait; let me tell you my story. When I was young, my grandfather abused me."

Sarah's eyes widen.

"He was nice at first, very affectionate, kissing and cuddling me all the time. He called me his special girl." Jenny swallowed.

"This is hard, so bear with me. I have a reason for telling you this." She blows her nose.

"One day he put his hand under my skirt and touched me there."

Sarah put her hand over her mouth.

"It got worse," Jenny told her.

"I hated him so much and ran away when he came to look after me. I was eight at the time, a little girl." Her voice sounds as though she is going to cry.

"Did you tell your mother?" Sarah said.

"She refused to listen. I was frightened. I even cut myself." Jenny showed small scars on her stomach.

"Of course, Grandfather denied everything. He said I was being spiteful because he had scolded me." Jenny wriggles two feet in the sand.

"Now I am older, I understand Mother had to choose who to believe, me—and deal with the consequences—or grandfather. She could not believe her own father would abuse a child." She looks in the distance.

"My mother was a struggling single mother who depended on Grandfather for money and babysitting." Jenny flushed.

"As an adult, I understand her position, but I hated her, too."

Neither of them spoke, focused on the waves breaking on the sand.

"One day, I saw a child screaming fit to burst when a bigger child tried to hit her. The bully child backed away. And it gave me an idea. Every time

Grandfather touched me I would scream at the top of my lungs." Jenny brushes the sand from her hair.

"Stop or I'll call the police," I yelled."

"I had to do this a few times. He stopped."

"Grandfather got the message."

A dog runs joyously along the beach, ears out, tongue rolling.

"I specialized in adolescent social work to understand my own issues," Jenny said.

"When I screamed at Grandfather, the self-harm stopped." She holds Sarah's hand.

"Your parents are enmeshed with Rachael and her drug use. I think they may have forgotten they have two daughters."

Sarah opens her mouth and a tsunami of words falls out.

"Rachael's injecting heroin. She almost died of a heroin overdose. I was so scared. She steals from everyone. Dad put a lock on my bedroom door when I caught her stealing my things. He has a padlock on the garage, a safe in the bedroom." Sarah takes a breath.

"Mother spends all her time taking Rachael to doctors and all sorts of treatment and counselling. Even detox." She is silent.

"Rachael doesn't want to stop. It's horrible at home." She starts crying.

Jenny hugs her.

Jenny fiddles with her silver bracelet.

"It's hard for your mum, she wants everything

perfect. A drug-using daughter implies deep problems in a family. She has kept Rachael's drug use a secret. It is difficult for your dad, too."

They sit in companionable silence.

"No one knows how to deal with a child dependent on heroin. It is all strange. Parents learn as they go, what works and what doesn't."

The setting sun turned the sky red and orange.

"Mrs Gilbert, my teacher at school, is helping me apply for an overseas scholarship, to study Anthropology in Cambridge." She hesitates, her eyes glisten.

"Now you know my secret plan."

"Rachael may stop using heroin or not. However, you must live your own life, not in the shadow of Rachael's."

She gives Sarah's hand a squeeze.

"Be tough and with a loud voice. Every time you think of cutting, scream instead." She has a gleam in her eye.

"That will shake up Paula and Colin. Ring or text me, we can scream together."

She laughs.

"And keep a diary; it helps to blow off steam. Even now, I always jot a few things every day to clear my head."

A parrot squawks in a nearby tree. They look up.

"When we return home, let's do something together like jazz dancing classes. Anyway, I need the exercise. You can keep me motivated. I will pay for the classes."

"You girls are the closest to daughters I'll ever have. My priority is to be there for you. Paula is hell-bent on rescuing Rachael, but it never works. The person with the addiction has to want to stop." Jenny brushes the sand off her bathers.

"I intend to take Paula to a support group called Family Drug Help, where they teach family members how to set boundaries."

"Show me the emu," Jenny said getting up.

That night Jenny and Sarah share a fish banquet under the stars. They join a group of women wearing hula skirts, dance and sing loudly until exhausted.

TWENTY-THREE

Whose fault
December 2005

"THIS WHOLE HEROIN MESS IS YOUR FAULT." COLIN jabs at Paula.

"You are always rescuing Rachael."

"Do you want her to die to prove your idiotic point?" Paula said.

"You're angry all the time. Can't you see the effect you are having on Rachael and Sarah." She exhales. "Sarah is self-harming."

"What?" Colin stands motionless.

"You heard me." She pulls a tissue from her pocket.

"I'm dealing with the issues and where are you? You are either hidden in the garage or at the pub with Max." She stands firm.

"So, blame me for Sarah. It's always my fault." She said.

"Why haven't you told me?" He said.

"Jenny said we spent too much time on Rachael and overlook Sarah."

"I told you were too soft on Rachael," he said.

"It is a waste of time trying to talk to you." Paula runs out of the room, slamming the door behind.

A little while later, she hears Colin's car drive off.

Paula pours a full glass of red wine and perches on the back step. Heavy metal music seeps from upstairs. Rachael's voice rises, echoing the singer's words of hate, death, and destruction.

She's high.

Ten minutes later, she is aware that Rachael is standing behind her.

"Can I sit next to you?"

Paula makes room on the step.

"I have been thinking that I might try the Suboxone program again," said Rachael.

"I am glad," Paula holds her tight.

When Colin returns, they are still sitting on the back step with their heads touching. He steps past them without saying a word.

He opens a beer. Flicks on the television, someone in Tasmania named Martin Bryant shot and killed thirty-eight people for no reason.

TWENTY-FOUR

Level-headed in a crisis
December 2005

FRIDAY NIGHT AT 11:30 P.M., PAULA AGAIN PULLS ON the black coat to search for Rachael. She plans to go to Woolworth's near Newmarket station. Last time she searched for Rachael she was there with two other girls.

There is a knock on the door. She checks her watch. It is late.

Two police officers stand illuminated under the porch light. One is older with grey hair; the other taller is younger.

"Mrs Wilson can we come inside?" The older police officer's voice is flat, matter of fact, business-like, His face like stone.

"We found a girl who resembles your daughter Rachael at the back of Woolworth's supermarket," said the police officer. He pauses. He tries not to look at her face, concentrating on her neck.

"I was just about to look for Rachael," Paula said. Her voice trails, she is aware that the officer's is trembling.

"Is your husband about?" He said.

Did Rachael try to break into the supermarket?

Paula calls Colin, who comes down the stairs fastening his dressing gown.

"Perhaps you both should sit down." The police officer's face is white.

Paula grasps Colin's hand. He puts his arm around her back. She cannot look at him.

The older police officer speaks slowly and with deliberation.

"I'm very sorry, Mr and Mrs Wilson; Rachael is dead."

He lets the words sink in.

This is the hardest part of his job. No matter how many times he has told a family member someone close has died either in an accident or misadventure, it always feels as though it is the first time. He hates this part of his job. People only hear the word 'dead.' Then shock sets in, denial, terror, wild emotions. He feels evil, destroying ordinary lives, breaking them, perhaps never to mend again.

He has a small boy at home and thinks of him as he stands telling another family their own beloved child is dead.

"We need someone to identify Rachael's body."

~

Rachael's death shines a spotlight on the Wilsons. The news runs like wildfire through friends, colleagues, and loved ones. "Accidental drug overdose," everyone shudders. It could have been anyone's daughter or son.

≈

The eulogies at the funeral mention Rachael's courage and personality. Barbara and Max speak of Rachael's joy of life. Trevor tells of playing computer games with Rachael. Her favourite music played in the background.

Colin, Paula, and Sarah are mute and too frozen to cry.

Paula rolls and unrolls the yellow ribbon with the raised red spots.

Colin looks straight ahead.

Friends and relations hold the family tight.

Emotions burn as acid.

The pain never abates.

TWENTY-FIVE

After the funeral
December 2005

PAULA LOVES THE GRITTINESS OF THE SAND AND THE soothing water.

There's something mystical and rhythmic in the vastness of the ocean and the ebb and flow of waves and tides.

Aunt Bertha lived next to St Kilda beach. When Paula was a child and visited Aunt Bertha, they always spent time at the sea building elaborate sand castles made of twigs and shells and watch the tide swish in and dissolve their works of art.

"That's life, my dear," said Aunt Bertha.

"Everything is temporary. You must enjoy every second."

Her beloved husband Walter died in World War II. The next husband, Des, died from a tainted blood transfusion on their third wedding anniversary.

"They were wonderful men," she said.

~

After Rachael's funeral, Sarah and Paula take some of Rachael's ashes to Indented Head beach intending to have a memorial in her honour. The rest of the ashes are stored at the Memorial Garden in Springvale.

Colin buries himself in work and refuses to accompany them.

Today, four seagulls form a semi-circle around Paula and Sarah. A tall seagull cocks a head at them, willing them to feed him. Orange legs are half-submerged in the waves; they wash against stick bird legs. Another seagull lets out a cry and the group stalk away.

Paula and Sarah hire a boat for the memorial. They light small fat candles on cardboard and float them on the water; they drop the ashes near *The Ozone*. The candles sink into the water one by one.

"Swim Rachael," said Sarah.

"Dive deep, Rachael," said Paula.

Five pelicans spread out on the wheel of the old steamship, *The Ozone*. It is a favourite landing place. One bird spreads his wings wide, resembles a kite waiting for the breeze to come. Three men push a small, tinny boat out to sea, then jump in as the motor starts and speed away.

Paula searches the horizon. Silhouettes of tall buildings stand as statistical bar charts. If she had a pencil, she could connect the tops to make a line graph.

What a curious thing to think.

"Do you remember when we were young, and we hiked from Indented Head to St Leonard's?" said Sarah.

"We packed a picnic basket with boiled eggs, tomato sandwiches, and watermelon, and sang silly songs on the way." Sarah tilts her head.

"Once I had a cocker spaniel, his name was Fred. Fred, Fred wet the bed." She stops.

"My poodle's name is Snoopy; he snoops along the beach…"

"Yes, I remember," Paula said in a soft voice.

≈

Wednesday, Paula drives Sarah to Geelong station as she must return to Melbourne for school.

"Take care, precious girl. Ring me when you get home. Dad will pick you up from the station."

"Will you be okay?" asks Sarah.

"Yes. I need time alone."

On her way back to the beach house, Paula stops at the Portarlington Golf Club. She orders a meal of roast lamb and vegetables. While waiting for the meal, she watches a man pour coins into a pokie machine. On a whim, Paula places two coins in a machine and wins $50. The gold coins make a metallic noise as they stream out. She feels a small lift in her spirit.

The next day, Paula is back on the beach. Dark clouds hover over the horizon and menace the shore. Dried seaweed sticks to her feet. The waves ripple as slow dancers, coming to the shore in unison.

Again, that night, she orders a meal at the Portarlington Golf Club and places 20 gold coins into a machine, this time winning $400 in a jackpot.

Everything in my life is madness, and this stupid machine gives me $400.

~

She returns to Westbourne Road. The house is full of withered flowers submerged in putrid water. Cards and sympathy notes pile on the kitchen bench.

How to keep on living?

~

Sarah wins the coveted scholarship to Cambridge University. It's enough for fees, accommodation, and a small weekly allowance. Colin pays the flight.

Sarah is radiant as she boards the Qantas flight to a new life.

She waves to her parents.

TWENTY-SIX

It's raining potato crisps
February 2006

COLIN LEAVES THE ROOM WHENEVER PAULA MENTIONS Rachael's name.

"I have no wish to rehash things," he said.

But Rachael is in his thoughts day and night.

~

He remembered Rachael at eight, mocking her grandmother.

"You will understand," Rachael had said, in a soft, measured voice, a hand in the air.

"I am not well, I must have my rest." Rachael clasped hands to her chest.

"I have not slept for a whole week, not for a minute."

With that, she rolled her eyes, and implored to the heavens with outstretched hands, feinted distress at the highest level.

"Don't forget the deep breathing," Colin said.

Rachael huffed.

They stopped laughing when Paula arrived.

"What's so funny?"

"Nothing..."

The garage smelled of burnt metal. Colin had been welding a bolt to a trailer. Turned the gas bottles on, pulled the goggles over his eyes.

"You have too many secrets," said Paula.

"We understand each other," he said.

Colin and Rachael were as two naughty children who kept confidences. They saw the world in a ludicrous way and mocked Paula with her measured kindness and sensibility.

"Everyone has their good points," Rachel used to say, using Paula's quiet voice and face to show sincerity.

"There are no wicked people, only unpleasant experiences."

Colin and Rachael exploded in raucous laughter.

~

Today, Colin scans the laptop perched amongst the soiled greasy rags and screws on the bench. Birds clomp on the roof. He stops, walks to the kitchen. Peers inside the fridge, cuts a generous slice of tasty cheese. Takes a packet of potato crisps and rests on the back step.

~

"Dad; look up," Rachael said those years ago.

He looked up to a hail of potato crisps falling on his head.

"It is snowing potato crisps; alert the media," she said, leaning out of the bedroom.

~

Colin crumples the potato crisp bag and returns to the garage, picks up a piece of equipment, cleans and polishes and adjusts the valve.

~

"What's that for?" Rachael had said, her hands greasy from handling his tools.

"When I grow up, I want to be an engineer like you and build things."

"Let's start with the billy cart."

They spent the morning measuring, cutting and drilling the base and fitted the wheels.

~

Today, Arpege perfume fills the garage.

"It makes no sense," said Paula.

"Don't preach. I'm not one of your students," he said.

They glare at each other.

"The trouble with you," she starts.

"You," he said, pointing to her, "never know when to shut up."

"You hide your feelings until they become toxic."

Paula walks around the garage, unsettled. She despises conflict.

"She was my daughter, too," he said, voice a deep growl. "Just because I don't sob and talk about her day and night."

"We need to talk through the feelings with a grief counsellor," Paula's face flushed, hates losing control.

"I'm dealing with Rachael's death my way."

"But you buried her in your life. It is as if she never existed," she said.

"How do you know? Can you read minds now?" Irritation shows on his face.

"You never mention her name. You haven't grieved," she said.

"I don't want to talk—"

"That's the trouble with you," she said.

"Bloody hell!" He spills the cup of coffee on the bench, storms out of the garage, doors bang, and a car starts.

We should separate. We're tearing each other apart.

Paula reaches under the bed for the small brown suitcase, throws assorted clothes into the case. She retrieves the black coat. Writes a note, leaves it on the kitchen table.

Have gone to Jenny's.

A one-word note has been pushed under the windscreen of her car.

Max's.

Paula replaces the suitcase under the bed, hangs the coat on the hook.

The house is silent. She pours a drink and presses the glass against her hot cheek. The ice clinks; the warmth of the alcohol disperses through her body.

Paula stands for a long time. She gazes out of the office window. She pushes the fringe from her eyes. She misses Sarah.

I wonder what you are doing Sarah?

Paula stares at the tall city buildings. They are golden and illuminated against the fading sunlight. The buildings reflect other buildings nearby, creating waves of yellow and glass. She thinks of the people living in buildings. Maybe they are looking out at her.

The streets are empty.

She waits for something to happen.

The landscape is dead space.

PART 2

TWENTY-SEVEN

Paula as a child
January 1968

"I PICKED THESE FLOWERS BECAUSE I LOVE YOU, Mummy," Daniel used to say.

"What a sweet boy," said Doris, her face shining.

It was lies. He feared Doris. He chewed his nails and shook at the sound of her voice. However, he had stumbled on Doris's weakness.

Paula studied Doris for clues that heralded a dangerous change in her moods.

"Come here," said Doris. Not to obey meant a double whack.

To the world outside Paula's childhood home, to the mothers and church groups; the family appeared perfect with quiet, obedient children and a caring husband. Doris's pleasant demeanour was on display for visitors. She paraded her children before an approving audience.

"You're a wonderful mother," they said.

Doris entertained Aunt Bertha and two women from the church; Paula was six and carried a tray of scones for the guests. Paula slipped, and the scones bounced onto the good rug, smearing it with raspberry jam and cream.

"Stupid girl," Doris leapt to her feet, shaking with anger. Her hand raised ready to strike.

"Look what you've done."

Paula screwed up her eyes waiting for the slap.

"Take the scones to the kitchen, bring the chocolate biscuits. And don't drop them," said Doris, her face etched in silent fury.

"And bring a wet sponge."

After the guests departed, the wooden spoon came out. Tartan slacks covered the bruises on her legs.

TWENTY-EIGHT

The camera
September 1968: Paula as a child

AUNT BERTHA CLIMBED ON A RICKETY WOODEN CHAIR and retrieved a large green hatbox from the top of the wardrobe. It was crammed with photos, old memories in marked envelopes.

"These are slices of my life," she said.

When Aunt Bertha opened the box, stories of the past cascaded out.

Paula's first camera, a brownie box, was her most prized possession. Aunt Bertha bought the camera for Paula.

"Always take photos," said Aunt Bertha.

"They will be the footprints of a life lived. The photos will remember even when the event fades from your memory."

"This is Doris and me." The black-and-white photo revealed two small girls with large side ribbons—one smiling, one not.

"Look at her scowling, always grumpy." She turned to Paula and grinned.

"I used to call your mother Miss Grumps."

"This is a photo of your mother and father on

their wedding day." She took off her glasses and polished them with the hem of her skirt.

"Stan looked so handsome."

She wrinkled her face.

Doris unsmiling carried an enormous bunch of flowers over her abdomen. A small hat perched sideways on her head, her eyes fixed on something out of camera range.

"Mother was skinny," said Paula.

"She became rounder after she had you and your brother."

"I never saw this photo."

"There were dramas going on at the time," said Aunt Bertha.

She patted Paula's hand. "I guess Doris didn't want to be reminded of them."

"This is Doris singing in the local theatre company. She had a lovely voice, contralto. I went to all of her concerts." She shook her head.

"Pity she stopped singing."

"I never knew Mother could sing."

"Your father used to hang around backstage. That's how they met."

She became quiet, she closed the hatbox.

TWENTY-NINE

The old woman pushing the trolley
April 2007

IT IS SIXTEEN MONTHS SINCE RACHAEL DIED. THERE IS a return of some resemblance of the old life for Paula and Colin.

Sarah is studying at Cambridge.

It is a wintry Sunday; the wind howls when the church door opens. Rain smashes against the stained-glass windows. St Paul's Cathedral is packed with worshippers.

Paula sits tightly between two women in a wooden pew near the back.

The woman next to Paula leans towards the man sitting by her side.

"What did he say?"

"He was brought as a lamb to the shearer, was silenced," he said.

A small dark-haired young girl whose large electric wheelchair straddles the aisle, smiles. Paula nods.

That chair must be difficult to manage.

People shuffle in their seats, there is a scraping of feet, wooden pews move as people stand and sit.

The priest's booming voice fills the spaces in the cathedral.

"I am crucified with Christ. Therefore, I no longer live. Jesus Christ now lives within me. Go to the entire world and preach the gospel, be baptised as a believer."

A tall thin man steps to the pulpit and communicates his conversion to Christianity. He speaks in Arabic. Another man translates his words into English.

A girl of four with dark Shirley Temple curls fidgets in the pew in front. She stands on the pew and pulls faces at the worshippers.

"When is he going to stop talking?" she asks in a loud voice.

A woman hushes her.

"Tell him to be quiet," the girl said.

The mother hauls the child out of the pew. They return a few minutes later. The girl is pouty and silent. She climbs on the pew and pokes a small pink tongue at Paula, who is tempted to return the gesture.

What a brat.

The priest returns to the elevated pulpit. "Judge not," he said.

"Miracles happen when it's inconvenient. You must practice your faith."

Easy for you to say, thinks Paula.

When the service ends, Paula lights three small white candles. She cups each candle's flame until it flares brightly. The flames flicker and cast a warm glow in the now-deserted cathedral. Stained glass windows stream colour beams to the empty pews.

This is a sacred space.

She prays for Rachael and her father, and those that struggle in life, says a prayer for the girl in the wheelchair.

May there always be good people to support her.

The force of the wind pushes her backwards as she struggles to open the door. She grips her coat tight.

It has stopped raining.

The street smells of rotting food and stale oil. Feet trample past in shoes, some in thongs, and sneakers. An old woman shuffles nearby. She wears a wide-brimmed floppy hat that covers brown, dangling hair.

She mutters, "I told him, but he said, 'No.'"

She pushes a wire shopping trolley laden with faded newspapers, covered with a pink towel. The wind stirs the leaves and threatens the trolley. She halts every few minutes, fiddles with the papers, and tucks in the towel. She limps and grimaces in pain.

Cans clatter and roll bits of paper blow into her face. The woman lurches side to side, the left foot points outward, and the right drags. Her dress stretched over a bulging body. Black socks that are half-masted show scratched legs and her glasses are lopsided on her nose.

The woman stops often, mutters to herself, "No," he said, "No way."

It must be hard for her to survive on the streets, thinks Paula.

Two young girls laugh, turn back to stare as the woman staggers to a seat dragging the trolley, rearranges the towel.

Where is she going?

The bells of St Paul's Cathedral peal. Paula trails the old woman to Flinders Street station. An assortment of youth sprawl on steps, others throng in groups. Trams clang. Young boys on bikes *swish* past making streams of flying water. Loud, booming male voices explode. Four girls hoot and shove.

Paula pretends to gaze at a shop window of assorted men's hats.

The woman parks her trolley at the bench. Five minutes later, she lumbers towards a group of scruffy males further down the street. One man hacks and spits into the road. They form a queue at the counter of a food van. The light of the van illumines a round-faced attendant.

"Hello, Johnny, me love, how's your flu? Did you see the doctor?" the attendant asks.

"He said I should stop the fags or they'll be the death of me." He grins a toothless smile.

"Have a cup of hot soup to warm you."

She hands a cup of bubbling tomato soup, a bun, and one sausage roll. He holds the soup, sips the warming liquid. Moves off eating the bread, pockets the roll.

I should volunteer with the homeless, thinks Paula.

"Mary, how are you?" The attendant asks the old lady with the trolley of newspapers.

"My legs hurt," she said.

Paula props against the Flinders station ticket barrier. She watches the old woman sip the soup and experiences a strange tenderness towards her.

Should I give her money? Does she have a family? Someone must have loved her.

We are both outsiders watching the normal world.

~

When Paula returns home, Colin is not there. This is the opportunity she has wanted.

She has a chore to do. Beads of sweat develop on her forehead.

Get going.

She fills the kettle and waits for it to boil, pours a small quantity of table salt into a cup and shivers.

I hate this.

Paula dampens an index finger, dips it in salt, then inside her mouth. Pauses. Within seconds the pain starts, searing, stinging. She clenches her teeth.

"God, oh God," she calls out in a hoarse whisper. She rocks back and forth.

When the stabbing sensation subsides, she dips the digit again, placing it over three bleeding mouth ulcers. The agony tracks up to the jaw. Salt and saliva swell. She spits in the sink, turning it red with blood.

She grasps the basin as waves of excruciating stinging agony overcome her.

This is torture.

She collects the boiled water, pours it into the cup with more salt. She sips it, swishes, holds the solution until she cannot endure it any longer, and spits it out. Red blood flows in the sink, she continues rinsing.

She clutches the basin.

Tears track her face.

Oh my God.

Paula will repeat this procedure several times a day over the next few days, until the ulcers soften and disappear.

Every second or third month, there is another outcrop of ulcers. She tried many therapies prescribed by doctors, chemists, dentists, and naturopaths. Nothing works except the salt.

Once she hadn't treated the ulcers fast enough, they multiplied and spread, covered inner cheeks and tongue. It took weeks of agonizing salt treatment to fix them.

The toughest part is undertaking the treatment

without Colin's knowledge. She is horrified he might see her spitting blood and doubled up in pain. This image is not one she wishes to share with anyone.

Paula scrubs the bloodied sink and makes a cup of Earl Grey tea.

Her wedding ring tinkles against the porcelain cup. She mulls over the day and the church service.

Does the old woman have a safe spot to sleep?

The door clicks. Colin bursts home. He is all noise and cheerfulness and smells faintly of beer.

"These are a present from Max, fresh from his garden," he said.

Places a large parcel wrapped in newspaper tied with a rag into Paula's arms. A flush of bright yellow daisies shines up at her.

"They are beautiful," she said.

"Thank you."

She kisses him.

THIRTY

Doris and the outing
May 2007

"She's late again," mutters Doris.

"That daughter of mine does nothing right."

She sits on her wheeler. Her face creases in a scowl.

Pictures of tasteful country scenes hang on the walls. The residents' voices rise and fall in tune to a sing-along in the recreational room.

Doris refuses to join them. The aroma of warm scones permeates the air.

"Give Paula a ring; tell her I'm waiting," Doris says to a passing nurse.

"Mrs Parker, it's early, not eleven."

"What do you mean it's not eleven?" asked Doris.

"The time is 10:30 a.m.," said the nurse.

"Ring Paula and tell her to get here now." Doris's voice rises in anger.

"I will if she hasn't come by eleven," said the nurse.

Doris pulls a face, shoves the wheeler to the

entrance. She sits at the entrance waiting. When the doors slide open, she glowers at Paula.

"You're late."

"It's not eleven."

"Don't argue with me, girl."

Here we go again. Why do I bother? Paula sighs.

"I bought you Rachael's pink Peony roses. Aren't they charming?"

"Rachael, that's all I ever hear from you. I'm the one suffering. As if you cared."

She throws the flowers on the basket of her wheeler.

It's going to be a long day.

"The roses are gorgeous," says the nurse.

"I'll put them in a vase for you." She winks at Paula.

"Your mother's been looking forward to her outing today." She smiles at Doris. "Haven't you, Mrs Parker?"

"I'm alone in this terrible place and punished by the likes of you." She jabs a finger at the nurse.

"Now that Sarah is overseas, and Rachael is dead, there's no reason why I can't live with you again." Her voice becomes louder and shriller.

"I demand you take me to live with you. I demand it." She stamps her foot. She lowers her voice. "Otherwise you won't get one cent from me."

That old threat. Daniel and I pay for everything.

"Did you tell Paula that your son Daniel and his wife visited yesterday?" She smiles at Doris.

"They took you to Highpoint. Didn't they Mrs Parker? And Julia bought you a pretty dress." The nurse adjusts the collar on Doris's cardigan.

"It wasn't a nice dress," Doris said.

"It was a cheap polyester one with pleats. I hate pleats and hate polyester. I threw it in the bin when they left. It was a horrible day. They made me sit in the back seat of the car. The food was terrible at the food court."

"How's Daniel?" asks Paula, trying to change the subject.

"Daniel is Daniel."

"You can sit in the front seat of my car today. I organized an appointment to have your hair done and we'll have lunch."

Doris is manoeuvred into the front car seat.

"I want the seat further back. The seat belt is hurting. The sun is in my eyes."

Paula switches the radio on. She turns the car into a disabled parking spot near the post office. She helps Doris out of the car and hands her the wheeler. They walk at a snail's pace towards the hair salon. It is a sunny Saturday afternoon. Crowds are milling on the street.

"Watch where you're going!" Doris hollers at a woman pushing a pram.

They nearly collide.

"I'm sorry," said the woman.

"No problem," said Paula.

"I'm mowed over by a pram and you take her side." Doris's voice rises into a rant.

Finally, they arrive at the hairdresser. Doris is ushered to the basin to have her hair shampooed.

This is such a waste of my time. I have sixty assignments to mark.

"Stop it, you are too rough. The water is too hot. Now it's cold. Don't pull my neck back," shouted Doris to the hairdresser.

Her hair is rolled into curlers and placed under the dryer.

"It's too warm. Turn it down. I don't like this magazine."

The hairdresser has an empty look on her face as she places Doris's head under the dryer.

Later when her hair is dry, "Watch what you are doing with the hairspray. It burnt my eyes. I do not like the way you set my hair. The front is not sitting right. You are the worst hairdresser I ever met."

Paula knows she will have to find another hairdresser.

They walk to the small cafe in Union Road.

Doris's foul mood continues in the cafe. She hates the toasted sandwiches; the cheese is tasteless.

Paula looks at her watch.

This is torture.

"My daughter put me in a nursing home," Doris said in a loud voice to no one.

The diners ignore her and keep eating.

Doris repeats her comments only louder.

"Time to go back," said Paula.

After she drops her mother back at the nursing home, Paula decides on a whim to check out the local pokies venue. While there, she does not think of Doris or Rachael and is transported to another world of bright lights and safety.

She wins $100, collects the money, and feels a little brighter as she drives home.

THIRTY-ONE

Locked in
July 2007

"GOOD HEAVENS," SAID PAULA ALOUD.

She pulls the car over to the curb for a closer look.

"It's my old home."

A small smile of pleasure creeps across her face at the sight of the familiar dilapidated house. She opens the car door and walks over.

There is a for sale sign leaning against a maple tree.

Demolition or Restore.

The old house is almost unrecognizable. Black tyres nudge out from withered weeds. Flaky thistles and overgrown grass flourishes in the front. Small yellow daisies spring on the side.

She creeps along the path. Her heart beats faster. Her breath coming in quick bursts.

I must watch out for snakes.

She peers through the dirt-encrusted windows. The back door is unsecured, thrusts it open. Immediately yelps and jumps when a torrent of debris falls on her head. Paula clamps a tissue to her nose. Shafts of patchy light gleam through the broken spaces in the roof. There is a sense of squatters. The place reeks of mildew. Two grimy mattresses and a torn blanket lie the floor. Hundreds of cigarette butts in one corner.

The place stinks.

She winces at the lingering stink of stale urine.

She steps on the curled edges of what is left of the green-and-white checked linoleum. A pile of yellowing newspapers, take-away food containers, and paper cups strewn throughout. Fossilized spiders adhere to ragged webs and sway as she passes. Ant colonies in single files travel steadfast through the rubbish.

'THIS LIFE IS SHIT AND THEN YOU DIE' is scrawled in black text on a wall.

What if someone is hiding here?

She loses her confidence, stops and calls out.

"Is anybody there?"

Her voice reverberates through the empty house. Listens. No sound. She recovers her self-control.

Paula shoves the back door open and blinded by sunlight. She treads the wooden steps, staggers when a step crumbles under her feet revealing obscurity beneath.

That was close.

Paula clutches the rickety banister. It sways and threatens to give way.

A mountain of smashed beer bottles slouches against a wooden fence.

A rusty Holden has collapsed, has no wheels. Doors wide open.

The old upright Hills Hoist swings in circles, the wires sagged and broken. Two pegs cling fast to a ragged, grease-streaked towel.

Mother would be heartbroken to see it.

The house and garden were always so neat. It's a mess now.

Paula shouts, "It's still here," and runs to the old peach tree. She laughs.

The tree has three round ripe peaches. She yanks the fruit, wipes it over her jeans, and bites hard on the fruit, juice drips from her lips, transported to another time when hot pies cooled on the kitchen table. A huge pile of peaches ready for bottling.

What happened to the Fowlers Vacola outfit?

She recalls carrying the bottled peaches to the storeroom.

The laundry cupboard. Is it still there?

She pulls herself up the steps. Finds the laundry.

She cries out when two terrified field mice flash past her legs.

The cupboard pretends innocence with its damaged door swaying on a hinge. It once existed as the family's storage space for bottled and preserved fruit and jams. It housed rows of shelves from floor to ceiling.

Paula's skin crawls at the thought of the

cupboard infested with insects. The collar of her shirt is soaked in sweat, her heart bounds.

≈

She remembers herself as a five-year child, pounding from inside the cupboard.

"Let me out. I'll be good."

It evoked images of her father's gentle voice murmuring outside the door.

"Be brave, Paula, it won't be long."

He never released her from the cupboard, no matter how much she begged. He was afraid of going against Doris's wishes.

"Jesus loves me this I know for the Bible tells me so." The words were fragments, something to hang on to as Paula as a little girl hunched in the enclosed space of the cupboard. She was sure they would find her dead. Ants over her face and in her ears and mouth, like the magpie she saw on the road.

When the time was right, her mother unlocked the door.

"Are you sorry now?" Doris said.

Paula nodded.

"I can't hear you. Do you want to go back in the cupboard?"

"I'm sorry," Paula said in a thin voice.

"Go to your room."

She ran to the bedroom with frilly flower

curtains, clutched Trixie her doll tight, and rocked, receiving comfort.

~

A magpie's song returns Paula from her trance to the present. She throws the half-eaten peach away and runs to the car.

In many ways, I am still locked in. I hate closed spaces. Hate lifts. The moment the lift door closes, I always memorise movie exits. Hate it when plane doors close, makes me feel entombed. I have the windows down when I drive. I know I drive people crazy with requests for open windows at work.

Paula hates to see any living thing in a cage. She musters self-control not to open cages in pet shops and let the animals free. Paula fashioned excuses not to take Sarah and Rachael to the zoo.

THIRTY-TWO

Sarah
August 2007 Cambridge

IT ALWAYS RAINS IN ENGLAND. A SOFT PATTERING stream of rain strikes the window. The darkness outside is broken up by the gleam of car lights sweeping past. In the building opposite, yellow lamplight illuminates rooms. Shadows of people traced in shade and light.

Sarah wears a long black t-shirt, sips green tea. She grins in the darkness.

I love being here.

She is happy, content now. At first, she found the move to Cambridge troubling. Being the new student from another country with no friends felt alienating. Her initial shyness suggested she was aloof, better than the other students. Eventually, she forced herself to make small talk and connect with the other students in the dormitory.

One day, a student named Buzz said during a tutorial, "I hear kangaroos bounce along the streets of Melbourne."

"Yes, we have a traffic lane for kangaroos," she said in a mischievous tone.

"People can be booked for traveling on that line without a furry pouch."

Later that day, Buzz and Sarah and four students met at the Swan and Duck for a beer.

"You have nice brown eyes, and I think I will call you Roo from now on."

Sarah snorted, "Roo, you have to be kidding," she said.

But Roo it was. Buzz refused to call her by any other name.

The other students called her Roo.

"Do you want to join us for a beer, Roo?"

At Cambridge, no one knew about Rachael.

Emails from her mother felt like a time warp. She mentioned Rachael in every email.

'Yesterday I drove to the Memorial garden and placed Rachael's favourite flowers on her grave,' wrote her mother.

Rachael did not exist in Cambridge; she did. Roo with the new spiky hairstyle developed the ability to down a pint of beer without drawing breath. She was a rarity; few Australians studied Anthropology there.

"Have you been to Ramsay Street?" They asked Roo.

The TV series "Neighbours" was popular in Britain. Sarah viewed the program for the first time in the student lounge and was bored by the show's blandness.

Buzz and Roo became close; they spent most

of their time together. Eventually became an item. They planned elaborate holiday vacations to the Amazon and sought to live with the natives. They both wanted to work for World Health Organization after they finished their study.

Buzz was tall with twinkling oriental eyes and a ridiculously high-pitched laugh. His father was Chinese, his mother Polish. Buzz's weird sense of humour reminded Sarah of her father.

"I think we should get married and have a child," he said.

"We could call him Cambridge after this old place."

Roo laughed; it was crazy talk.

They became awkward lovers but soon educated themselves about sex.

Roo spoke of her aloneness growing up in her family.

"Everything centred on Rachael. I was invisible most of the time. I couldn't get my Mother or Father's attention. Especially after the accident, and when Rachael used heroin, it was only about my sister. I felt an outsider," she said.

"I escaped from the shadow of Rachael by coming to Cambridge."

"I know what you mean. We are both escapees," he said.

"I left home because it was toxic. I picked Cambridge because it would be too far for them to visit.

"Father came out as a gay man. I had no problem with him being gay or even having a young lover. He always has been a cool father." He smiles.

"Father did all the midlife metaphor stuff; middle-aged man, excessive gym work, and younger paramour." He looks at Roo.

"What really bugged me was my mother's revengeful religiosity." He pulls a face.

"She kept saying to me, 'Your father is a sinner leaving his family and becoming a homosexual.'"

"Members of my mother's church stopped me in the street asking if my father was still walking with Satan," Buzz chuckles, mimicking a voice,

"We are all praying for his soul," said one man from my mother's congregation."

Roo once regarded her mother as strong, but now felt she was controlling like her Grandmother Doris.

"My mother's obsession with all things Rachael even in her death makes me feel creepy," Sarah said.

Buzz liked the sound of Colin, his jokes, and his sense of the ridiculous.

"I want to meet him." He said.

They lay on Buzz's bed, deliberated on useful programs that incorporated cheap loans for disadvantaged women to buy sewing machines in Nicaragua. They attended rallies that decried poverty. And opposed the global summit.

Buzz educated Roo on warm beer in tall glasses.

She invested in black bras with French lace and underpants to match.

Buzz supported this venture.

Previously Sarah secretly envied Rachael's wild behaviour. Sarah eyed authority figures with dread; her mother omnipresent, her father less so. She sought identity by being a high achieving student. Kept her bedroom tidy, remained polite. Her friends were like her, quiet and intelligent.

No one expected Sarah to have large dreams.

She slipped away overseas.

Even as the focus remained on the dead Rachael.

But Roo took risks, was joyful and loud.

THIRTY-THREE

The old black coat
September 2007 Newmarket

SUNDAY MORNING, PAULA YANKS THE OLD BLACK COAT from the sliding door cupboard. The coat hangers dance. She tugs at the gold chain around her neck, clicking the metal against her teeth. The chain had been a wedding anniversary gift from Colin who wrapped it in foil. He placed it in a small box at the bottom of her lunch bag. She almost threw it away with her lunch rubbish. Once, Colin enjoyed springing exaggerated surprises earlier in their marriage, but not now.

She pulls her ear lobe as if afraid it might float.

"My turn to see Mother."

"I can't understand why you cater to the old witch," he said, looking up from his breakfast.

Paula sees her mother at the weekend. Colin refuses to have anything to do with Doris.

She checks her reflection in the mirror, applies red lipstick. Her breathing quickens.

A stranger seeing her might be suspicious she is preparing to meet a lover.

Her eyes sparkle.

She reverses the car, being careful not to hit the wooden letterbox.

She does not drive to the nursing home, instead arrives at the shopping centre in high spirits.

Small groups of African women float by in colourful gowns of flaming red and gold. Tattooed men stand smoking. Couples push laden prams and cling to toddlers. Sullen boys trail behind parents. Elderly men and women steady themselves with walking sticks and frames. A queue develops around the fresh bread counter.

She makes a mental note to buy a Boston bun for Colin.

Paula strides through the glass doors, past the alcohol outlet and hairdressers, to the Tabaret. It is normally loud with machines singing out cheery notes, bells ringing,

"You have free games."

Now and then swearing and fists thumping machines, "Come on, come on."

Not today.

Sunday morning most punters are shopping, in bed, at church, picnicking with families, reading the Sunday papers.

She smiles, a flush of anticipation.

It is a lucky day.

She knows it in her bones.

Assorted flickering lights of red, gold twinkle on the ceiling. The carnival displays on the pokie machines are colours of the rainbow. A radio plays the Bee Gees' "Staying' Alive."

At the bar bench sits a jug of water circled with glasses.

High-backed stools stand behind each machine, neat and orderly. Only two punters in the venue. A stooped, grey-haired man with a walking stick propped on the machine.

"Oh dear, oh dear." He periodically mops his brow with a large handkerchief.

In a corner is a rounded woman. Three overflowing plastic grocery bags at her feet.

The punters press buttons, not looking up. They glare at the machines.

Internal blood pressures zoom up and down in time to the dance of the reels. When the free games come up, pupils dilate.

Nobody smiles.

Two attendants stand beside the wooden bar sharing a joke.

Paula positions herself at the Timber Wolf machine. She screws her nose at the lingering odour of cigarettes that drifts in as the door opens and shuts from the smoking room to the side of the gaming venue where three men smoke.

Why do people smoke when they know it is bad for them?

In the last few months, Paula has been gambling on and off. She views it as a harmless past time, a form of time out.

She has grown to love the Timber Wolf game with its winter snow theme. The hungry wolves howling, the men in fur hats, the three owls that herald free games. She delights as a child watching TV cartoons after school.

She feeds $50 into the slot, reels spin, then stop; images enticing, hypnotizing.

"Come on," she said, bangs on the machine.

The $50 disappears.

She slips another $50 in the slot.

The free games must come soon.

Takes another $50, then another. She searches her wallet, the money gone.

Paula reaches for the RESERVED FOR TEN MINUTES ONLY sign. It falls to the ground. She replaces it.

Paula marches through the two sets of sliding glass doors to the entrance to the supermarket. Shoppers surround the ATM. Cash registers open and shut. People lunge around trolleys piled high with plastic bags.

"Excuse me," Paula said, elbowing a woman out of the way.

"Such rudeness," said the woman glaring at Paula.

Paula withdraws $300 from her credit card from the ATM. Goes back inside, removes the reserved sign from The Timber Wolf game, and feeds $50 after $50. Her face flushes. Triples her bets and five howling wolves appear. She has the free games.

Come on, win big.

She experiences a rush of euphoria and gives an audible gasp of pleasure.

Pours a glass of water from the water jug. The coolness is soothing.

She wins $500.

Maybe I should collect the money and go.

Decides to stay, feels more luck is in store. Triples her bets. The luck does not materialize. She reduces her bets as the money evaporates.

Damn.

The Tabaret has filled, a growing cacophony of people noise and jarring perfume. Men argue over football matches as they lean over the bar. Those eager to part with their money search for a vacant machine.

Paula turns to a young woman with flowing black hair next to her.

"Can you keep an eye on my machine for five minutes?" Paula asks.

"Sure." The woman does not look up from her machine.

Paula remembers a woman hijacked her reserved machine. She watched in disbelief as the machine-thief won reel after reel of free games. The attendant asked the woman to leave. The machine high jacker grinned as she collected the winnings in a blue plastic cup.

"Paula," a voice rings out near the ATM.

"I thought it was you."

Paula shudders. The gossipy colleague from work captures her, she drones on and on.

At first, Paula feigns interest, and then inspects her watch.

"I must go," said Paula with a forced smile, showing teeth.

"Next time we can have a long lunch and I can show the photos of my trip to Sweden," said the windbag.

"Yes, that would be nice," Paula said.

That is never going to happen.

Paula runs to the car. Stumbles in the bright sunlight, confused and disorientated.

She feels rattled by the staff member, somehow exposed. It has spoilt the day. Now has a knot of fear in her gut.

She drives as if drunk.

"Come on, move it. Watch where you are going?" She shouts at a slower driver in front of her.

At home, Paula's hands quiver. She drops the butter knife to the floor. Knocks over a glass of water. Sets eight slices of wholemeal buttered bread, waits for the waffle-maker to heat. Opens a can of baked beans for the filling and cooks lunch.

"How was the battle axe today?" said Colin over lunch.

"Same old Doris."

She mimics her mother's voice. "I am the one suffering in this dreadful nursing home. I demand you take me to live with you now." Paula stresses *demand* shaking her finger.

They both laugh.

THIRTY-FOUR

Madam Butterfly
September 2007 Melbourne

THE RED CARPET AT THE STATE THEATRE STRETCHES TO the bronze railing. Enormous abstract Australian paintings look down from the walls, splashes of red, blue, and yellow. Older women with granddaughters in tow move past. Women with towering high heels and long blonde hair cling to the arms of partners and leave a dense trail of Channel perfume. Middle-aged couples gossip together. Champagne glasses litter the marble side-tables.

Paula and Colin sink into the red plush armchairs.

"This is the life," said Colin. He sips the champagne.

"We are the hoi polloi."

He purchased the tickets for *Madame Butterfly* on the advice of Max.

~

Colin had confided to his brother that Paula was distant and often hard to contact at work.

"I wonder if she is seeing someone?" Colin said.

"Don't be stupid; she's probably thinking about Rachael and missing Sarah. You should take her out for a special treat." He looked at Colin.

"Even though it is expensive, take her to the opera." He nods to confirm his own words.

"Women love to cry. Makes them feel good. Barbara always enjoys a good cry."

～

"Look at the stars on the roof." He points.

The room fills with music as the orchestra warms up.

"You're as lovely as a garland of flowers," came from someone in the row behind.

Colin cranes his head to look.

"No garland of flowers. Very plain," he whispers to Paula.

"Welcome to *Madame Butterfly*. Please switch off your mobile phones," said a female voice. The lights dim, the curtain with the Australian lyrebird motif opens.

The story of Madame Butterfly is a tragic tale set in Japan. Lieutenant Pinkerton gains a beautiful fifteen-year-old geisha wife, Madame Butterfly, from a marriage broker. There is family opposition to this union. At one stage, an uncle bursts in on the stage cursing Butterfly for renouncing her ancestor's religion by marrying Pinkerton. He orders priests and family to leave his home. Then leaves Butterfly and returns to work in the navy, promising he will return.

The opera creates a crack in which human emotions open and experienced. The dark side of the soul is embodied in the opera.

The patrons, sob, others sit breathless, surrendering to the deepest part of the heart and emotion.

At interval, long queues line up for champagne and ice cream. Colin buys ice creams and they lick them contently.

"I don't understand why the story was not made in English." Colin said.

"I have a cramp in my neck looking up at the translation."

Paula laughs.

Women rush for the toilets. Within five minutes, the toilet line snakes out from the door. The bells ring and they return to their seats.

For a long time, Butterfly waits patiently for Pinkerton despite the negative comments of her maid. The aria *One fine day* tells of Butterfly's hopefulness. One day, Pinkerton's ship is seen in the harbour. Butterfly is full of joy. She rushes into the room full of youthful expectation and realizes the foreign wife of Pinkerton is next to Pinkerton.

The audience knows that tragedy will be the

outcome. Butterfly says goodbye to her son and stabs herself.

"Butterfly, Butterfly," is the call as she dies.

The audience feels Butterfly's agony.

Her grief is their unhappiness.

They endure the stab wounds and are depleted.

The audience connects with memories of their own; enjoys elation and crushing defeat and sorrow.

Paula sobs.

"It's only a story," Colin said. He is alarmed. "I wanted you to be happy."

"I am happy," Paula blows her nose, tears glistening on her face.

"Thank you for the opera. I loved it. It is so beautiful."

She bent over and kissed him his cheek.

I will never understand women as long as I live. He thought.

THIRTY-FIVE

McDonald's and the train
October 2007 Melbourne

"Bastards, bloody bastards," said the man as he threw his jacket on the chair.

He yanks the white sneakers off his feet and tosses them.

"Fuck you all."

His fear is a snake, eating him, wrapping around, squeezing. He slumps in the chair. McDonald's is a journeyman to his pain.

People move to make a space around this strange man. Others look from their burgers and fries and dart anxious eyes towards him.

The man becomes quieter. He licks his Pensioner's Special vanilla ice cream, savouring the coldness and sticky sweetness. Hair shock white, combed, and slicked. Wears a clean checked red-and-blue shirt and brown corduroy pants. Resembles a stick insect perched on the chair, making tiny smacking sounds.

The man replaces feet inside the sneakers,

grabs his jacket. Stands, shoves hands into trouser pockets, head bent down, and shuffles out.

He stops at the exit, unsure where to go next, turns to the left, stops, goes to the right. Bewildered, he disappears as though evaporated into the night air.

Paula holds her cup and watches from her seat.

Poor confused man. When I was a new social worker and worked at The City Mission years ago, there were many such broken men, shouting and staggering.

She remembered one client at City Mission who always smelled of alcohol and stale tobacco. His wrinkled withered face could be any age. Life had disfigured him. He spent nights sleeping out in the rain with bits of cardboard for cover. One eye perpetually open for the idiots who enjoyed hassling a homeless person.

"I have an appointment," he said to the woman at the front desk.

"Hello, Mick, come to my office," Paula said.

Her work spot was a tiny room with a desk jammed against the wall and two chairs. It was almost 6 p.m., and she wanted to go home. It had been an unending day of people with personal issues.

"What seems to be the problem?" she said.

"I want to send my Jilly a birthday card today. Can you write something for me?"

He held out a card with roses. "What shall I say on the card?"

"Happy birthday, Jilly. Dad says hello." He stops.

"Add a few words telling her I broke my glasses and that's why you are writing the card for me." He dived into a pocket.

"Put this $5 in with the card so Jilly knows her Dad still loves her."

"Do you have the address?"

He shook his head.

"I could take you to the house but don't know the number."

"Let's check the white pages on the computer."

She locates the address, writes it on the envelope.

"Do you have a stamp?" She knows he hasn't.

"I can provide one."

She promises to post it on her way home.

These homeless fellows always amaze me; just when you thought you know them, they show their soft underbelly.

Full of bravado and brashness.

Despair leads many to alcohol. So many like Mick.

∽

Today there are long queues, the teenagers behind the McDonald's counter run back and forth, collecting fries, hamburgers, and soft drinks. The customers turn their heads upward as if in a church, looking up at the florescent screen altar showing the day's specials.

Boys fiddle with phones. A baby pusher squelches as it moves, cash registers ping.

A small girl skips in excitement.

"One Dinosaur Children's Meal, cheeseburger, small fries, and a chocolate sundae."

She grins, "Don't forget my Smurf gift."

The tables are bolted to the floor. Sparrows invade and claim any leftover scraps.

"Twinkle, twinkle little star," a toddler sings. She makes star shapes with baby hands. An Asian woman joins the song.

A bored father shares a table with three boys.

"Come on, come on. We haven't got all day."

The boys fiddle with the burgers, slurp colas.

"I have to go to the toilet, Dad." The boy fidgets in his chair, wriggling back and forth.

Rachael always wanted to check out other people's toilets.

"I have a billy cart," said a young boy, his face covered in freckles, to Paula.

"What colour is it?" Paula said.

"Red and white. Would you like a ride in my billy cart?"

A woman rushes up, "Is he annoying you?"

Paula laughs and shakes her head. "He says he has a billy cart."

"Grandpa hasn't finished building it yet. Say goodbye to the nice lady."

"Bye."

Colin and Rachael built a billy cart. I wonder what happened to it?

Paula inspects her watch, the train due in fifteen minutes. She pulls the black coat over her shoulders.

Outside, weary horses carrying tourists, clatter up and down Swanston Street.

The city is invaded by tattooed men and women. Bored police move around in pairs.

At Flinders Street railway station, relentless feet march up and down stairs and escalators to the symphony of announcements related to departures and delays.

"The Graigeburn train leaves in five minutes from platform five," a disembodied voice said.

On the opposite track, a diesel train screams through without stopping. Sounds of steel over steel, *clicky-clack*. Empty aluminium cans roll back and forth in the carriage. Men wear thick parkas and women sport a variety of coloured scarves around necks.

Paula's train arrives, she scrambles on board, finds a window seat.

A grey-haired woman knits. As her station approaches. she pushes the needles into a brown ball of wool, wraps the knitting in a blue scarf, and places it in the basket at her feet.

"Won't be long. We left Flinders street station so be there soon," said a female talking on her phone.

One girl carries a heavy knapsack. Her purple hair pulled back, wears scholarly glasses and a nose ring.

Most passengers appear engrossed with mobile phones.

A boy eats fries splashed with tomato sauce from a cardboard container.

The train rocks back and forth, hurtles through tunnels, darkness, then flashes of light, then dark. Neat homes come into view.

Beep, beep, the pneumatic sound of doors opening, *Beep, beep* as they shut.

∼

Earlier that evening, Paula, Jenny, and Adriana met for dinner at Southgate to celebrate Adriana's birthday. They decide on a Greek restaurant. Paula as usual, is the first to arrive, then Jenny who chatters on about her latest sweetheart. She relishes the freer rules of dating and men find her attractive. She wears her hair short, tight jeans, and breast-embracing cleavage.

Paula enjoys hearing about Jenny's love life. A nice distraction from her own.

"How're things with you?" asks Jenny.

"How's Sarah?"

"Sarah loves Cambridge. I wonder if she'll ever come back." They laugh.

Have envy for the young with their endless travel opportunities.

Adriana arrives, full of apologies for being late. They hand her ribbon-bound parcels.

"Happy birthday, darling" Paula and Jenny said.

Adrianna opens the parcels and squeals with delight.

"Oh, I love these."

Paula and Jenny have both given coloured scarves.

"I love the scarves; they suit my new red winter coat," she said, giving each a hug.

They have shared many such meals over the years. There is always amicable talk and laughter. They have been a witness to each other's younger selves. No matter how old they become, they still see each other in the prism of youth when they met.

After the meal, they drift off in dissimilar directions. Jenny to meet Bob. Adriana's husband arrives to collect her. He does not want Adriana riding the trains at night.

Paula leaves alone.

∽

Paula leans against the train window. She

reminisces about the rowdy student parties the three friends shared when they were at university. It was an alternative lifetime.

Her life now divided into two parts: before Rachael died and after.

A void in between.

It is easy to slip into the emptiness.

THIRTY-SIX

The roses
October 2007

Such strange weather. I wonder why the rose leaves are black and withered?

Last night, Paula dreamed she wore the pink frothy dress with two petticoats that Aunt Bertha made for her sixth birthday. It had a swirl skirt and white sash and rustled. She swished around and around until she was giddy.

When she woke, the happiness enveloped her momentarily.

Then she remembered.

Rachael was dead.

THIRTY-SEVEN

Sarah's email
October 2007

EACH MORNING, PAULA CHECKS HER EMAILS FOR NEWS from Sarah. The emails tell of a new life that Paula will never experience.

"I have a boyfriend. You will like him. His name is Buzz. I'll send photos soon. I will not be able to email for a few days: we are off camping. The following weekend, four of us have organised a bus trip to Wales. When are you and Dad coming to visit? I want you to meet Buzz."

"Soon," Paula answers.

The reality is, she can barely pay the minimum of her credit card debt each month.

THIRTY-EIGHT

The staff meeting
November 2007

THE TABLES IN THE MEETING ROOM FORM A RIGID square. There is space on either side of where the Head of School is sitting. No one wants to be near the Head of School, neither to left nor right. Both sides are dangerous.

He has a habit of turning to persons on either side and directing them to carry out menial tasks.

"Photocopy this document and pass around to the group."

He has a secretary who takes the minutes, but she is too valuable to have running here and there on demand. He treats the academic staff with disdain. Is skilful at stabbing with words. The first blow comes from him. This controls the others. He prides himself of getting things done but in reality, creates chaos and unpleasantness.

Uses charm to get his way from those who are of use to him, those higher up the academic chain. And scornful towards those under him.

Paula is fearful of the Head. She has heard the stories. A colleague was overlooked for promotion after she argued with the Head. Another who disagreed with him was forced to undertake the arduous task of student selections at the start of the year. This meant no summer break holidays.

The new academics are clustered together as though there is strength in numbers.

One staff member asks a difficult question that appears to challenge the Head's authority. There will be punishment. He has a long memory.

The meeting room is hazy with unexpressed anxieties.

The Head takes off his glasses, makes a few niggly points showing his displeasure. He has small beady eyes, shrunken in face. Does not meet anyone's gaze, stares above people. Teeth clench as he speaks.

A popular staff member has resigned. An unpopular staff member has been elevated to her role. She has few skills to do the required work but is an expert at manipulation. Has learnt to feed the Head's insecurities. She tells him tales of staff who leave early or come in late.

The Deputy Head speaks, her voice unsteady, apologetic.

"Staff appears to be unhappy that normal due process changed," she said. She casts her glance to everyone in the room.

"We had no time, we had to make a quick decision," she said.

The Head chews his nails, he interrupts,

changes the topic. He continues with deliberate words that imply threat.

"I'll allow five minutes for comments. Be brief. I have to leave for a meeting with the Dean."

Paula glances at the others.

They sit wooden with fury, staring at each other across the room with grim faces.

"I would have liked to apply for the position," said a tall, red-headed woman.

The Head is uninterested, glances at papers in front of him.

"You don't have the management skills for the position," he said through closed teeth.

"Even though you may think you have."

He expresses the words with malice, chiselled to stab and hurt.

They reach the target.

The red-haired woman storms out of the room.

"Any further comments?" He said.

No one speaks.

"Right. I'll leave for the Dean's meeting."

As soon as he leaves the room, everyone speaks at once.

The Deputy attempts to regain order, endeavours to return to the general business.

"Let's run through the remaining agenda items and people can comment at the end." Dissenting voices rise and fall.

One staff member shouts, "This is so wrong on every level."

The Head abruptly reappears, motions the Deputy, whispers in her ear and disappears.

"The meeting is cancelled. Write any comments and pass to the Head's secretary," said the Deputy.

What possessed me to leave my satisfying work as a social worker and become an academic in such a brutal environment?

On the way home, Paula spends an hour at the Tabaret and loses $200.

THIRTY-NINE

Doris's illness
November 2007

"Your mother is in the hospital and wants you," said the nurse at Doris's nnursing home.

She looks at her watch. It is 3 a.m.

Paula dresses and drives to the hospital. She can hear her mother yelling as she enters the cubicle.

"Paula, Paula!"

"I'm here."

"You took your time getting here." Doris's face obliterated with an oxygen mask.

"Get this thing off me."

A nurse materialises as an alarm goes off.

"Keep the mask on; it'll help you breathe." She replaces the elastic around Doris's head.

I wish I could feel something for this woman, but there have been too many years of torment.

I hate hospitals. How many times did I end up at the hospital with Rachael? Three? Colin once. Now Doris.

"I am reluctant to admit Mrs Parker to the ward as we have few beds. As soon as she is stable, she will return to the nursing home." said the doctor.

Paula sits on the chair next to her mother's trolley in the emergency department overnight, mostly watching her sleep. Every so often, she walks around to stretch. A nurse offers her an instant coffee.

"Please stay with your Mother, she is quite apprehensive, and we are short staffed," said the Nurse.

How am I going to function at work tomorrow?

Every so often Doris wakes and shouts, "Paula, Paula..."

"I'm here; everything is all right. Go back to sleep."

She rings Daniel at 8 a.m. He arrives puffy and red-faced.

Paula goes home for a quick shower and meal. When she returns, Doris is in short-stay ward, sitting out of bed, no oxygen mask.

Doris holds Daniel's hand, delivers a weak smile.

FORTY

The safe deposit box
December 2007

"Mrs Wilson, your Mother died in her sleep," said the nurse from the nursing home.

Paula clung to the phone unable to breathe.

"Thank God she's gone; we can have our lives back," said Colin.

~

Paula, with assistance from Daniel, organises Doris's funeral. Distant relatives are contacted, a coffin chosen, flowers picked. They decide on cremation. Doris's ashes are placed in a small box next to a rose bush at the east side of the Springvale Memorial Garden Cemetery.

Stan's ashes in the west side.

"Poor Dad. He suffered so much with Mother. It's fair that she is separated from him in death," Daniel said.

After the funeral, an elderly aunt visits Paula and hands her a parcel.

"Doris instructed me to give you this after she dies."

The parcel revealed a brown leather school satchel. It contained childhood mementos made by Paula and Daniel. Hand-painted childish drawings, Mother's Day cards with lace written in scrawly writing. Locks of baby hair tied with ribbon. Baby teeth in a small jar and pink and blue baby shawls.

I am surprised she kept anything from our childhood. Perhaps at some level she loved us. Though she never showed any indication she had warm feelings for us.

When Doris's Will is read, it contains another surprise. A fixed deposit box reveals $100,000 in blue stock shares and cash squirreled away for years. It is shared equally between Paula and Daniel.

"We can use the money to reduce the mortgage on our house, said Colin.

Paula agrees, but is privately unhappy; she had intended to clear her credit card debt with the money.

Her credit card debt has increased to match her fascination with the pokies.

FORTY-ONE

Colin in Perth
December 2007

ON ONE OF THE NIGHTS THAT COLIN WAS AWAY IN Perth on business, Paula's lucky break came in.

'Congratulations, you have won a jackpot of $5,000.'

Paula stared in disbelief as the machine lit up and made wild cheerful noises.

Other patrons came over to see her screen.

A venue attendant hurries over. "Ohhh, that is wonderful. Let me have your driver's licence and I'll chase up the manager to write the cheque."

A random spin of the reels flooded her with happiness. She shone with pleasure as if she had achieved something marvellous. Ran a race and won. Discovered a cure for cancer. Starved her body for beauty.

The possibilities are endless. I could pay some of the credit card debt. Take Colin out for a slap-up meal. I won't tell him where the money came from. He detests gambling in any form. Send Sarah some money. Pity the win wasn't more so I could visit Sarah.

Colin is a man who prides himself on being frugal

with money. Paula on the other hand, is generous, buying treats and surprises for others. She is less generous towards herself. Has not bought clothes since Rachael died. Dislikes department shopping centres. Is more likely to buy a book than a dress.

She maintains a personal loan for her car and is still paying the loan.

Colin and Paula squabbled about money at the beginning of their marriage. They decided to hold separate bank accounts. The division of who pays what bills was established early and mortgage payments shared.

She waits fortnightly for the paycheque to come in and cover minimum payments to her credit cards and loan.

Paula believes Colin is the one with the problem with money. He uses money as power. Over the years she learnt not to ruffle his feathers about her finances; he is critical enough of her life.

He hates that she works in a university as an academic, is jealous of her confidence, never loses an opportunity to grumble of the time and effort she spends on her university work.

Tonight, while waiting for the cheque to be written, Paula relives the feelings of the random jackpot win. She is ecstatic. Smiles broadly to herself. Looks at her watch, is surprised to see it is 11 p.m.

Time has passed so quickly.

She came here after work. Has not had a meal. Is not hungry.

Thank goodness Colin is away; he would go ballistic if he knew what I was doing.

If Paula could see inside her brain she would notice the neurotransmitter dopamine surging through her brain networks. The surge is creating locked-in memories that will motivate her to repeat the effect. To gamble again and again to obtain that moment of euphoria. But she cannot see the process.

Paula experiences feelings of pleasure that she has not felt since Rachael died. One moment an ordinary woman but now happy.

The gambling snuck in as a light shaft in a darkened room. It became the fire and colour of her day.

The cheque arrives, she bounces out of the venue to her car.

Later when Paula was in bed at home, she turned the side lamp on, it cast a golden glow against the wall, made a flicker shadow on the ceiling.

Picks up a book from the side table. Puts it down.

Is wired, excited.

I wonder if there is anything interesting on the TV?

She feels out of place, an intruder, like someone who snuck in through an open window and was looking around. Notices a crack in the wall near the ceiling.

Was it there yesterday?

Am I going mad? What is that twisted, irrational part of me that drives me to gamble?

The gambling also gave Paula licence to lie. Paula had started to move around the venues, going to different ones. She did not want to be seen as one of the tragic ladies that came in often. Hated it when venue people recognised her or spoke to her. Vowed never to go again.

If a lonely person tried to talk to her, she would be evasive, rude not make contact.

She planned the gambling carefully. Every time Colin flew interstate on business, Paula stayed at the venues until late. Shocked and elated at how late it was, shivering in her black coat running for the car.

Getting home exhausted and overwrought, high as a kite, reaching for the whiskey, one or two or three shots to come down and stem the growing feelings of panic.

She told herself lies, why she gambled. She was sad, her husband did not understand, missed Sarah, was sad over Rachael's death.

Any reason to play the pokies.

The machines made her feel alive energised, a burst of energy. She was a willing partner to the dance. It all made sense, seemed the right thing to do at the time.

She rationalised that she did not rob anyone, it was her money, using her credit cards.

Tonight, she relived the $5,000 jackpot win; remembering every second, feeling the warm exhilarating pleasure. The jackpot sign coming on her machine, the announcement, "The jackpot of $5,000 has just gone off in this venue." She had looked in disbelief at her machine screen. She had won $5,000, the cheerful attendant smiling, "Congratulations."

It would be only a matter of time before she would win again.

She was sure of this.

FORTY-TWO

The hairdresser
February 2008

THE WALLS OF THE HAIRDRESSING SALON ARE PAINTED fire engine red. Huge ornate silver-framed mirrors hang in front of each salon chair. Pictures of impossibly beautiful women adorn walls. Paula wriggles on the salon chair, stares at the walls.

The photos must be enhanced. No real woman looks like that.

Mobile phones ring, "Can't talk, getting my hair done," said one girl, her head covered with long strips of silver paper.

Several blow dryers roar. Clients are propelled from seat to rinse basins, and back. The acrid smells of perm solution, hair spray, and perfume mingle. The radio plays Rod Stewart.

Clippers zoom over the head of a youth. He has a new pink baldness, hair lying in sad tufts on the floor. Grins at his image in the mirror. Runs his hand over the hairless skull.

"Mum will have a fit."

"I know you." An angular woman leans towards Paula.

"I don't think so," said Paula, she recoils. The woman is in her space.

"My memory's good, I never forget a face," the woman moves closer. She is thin like a whippet dog, long legs and heavy sparking jewellery.

Paula turns to her magazine.

"I remember now," the thin woman said, she takes Paula's arm. "You sat next to me at the pokies the other night."

"You're mistaken," said Paula. A red flush growing up her neck, spreading to her face.

"No, I'm not." The woman's voice is sharp, brittle. "I know it was you, because you reminded me of that woman who beat John Howard at the election; Maxine someone. I forget her surname." The woman looks triumphant. "Oh, I get it," she said, bursting into laughter. "You don't want to admit you play the pokies. Two-bit snob. High and mighty."

The buzzer next to Paula rings, the hairdresser whisks Paula to the basin, washes her hair vigorously. Paula turns to where the angular woman was sitting. Sighs with relief when the woman leaves.

"Do you know the woman? She seems to know you," said the hairdresser.

"No, she has me confused with someone else," said Paula.

Paula watches twin boys in identical blue striped tops punch at each other. A hairdresser sprays an older woman's hair. Clouds of sweet smelling hairspray rise in the air, holds up the mirror for the woman to see the back.

"Lovely, dear," said the woman.

This is the part Paula dreads, the endless cheerful chatter. As if on cue, Susan starts.

"Do you want a trim? How's the family?" She is tiny, a small ornate bird.

She wears enormous red, high-heeled sandals and has long dark hair. The phone rings and she darts to answer it, calling another hairdresser to finish.

"I'll be back to trim your hair. Do you want a cup of tea?"

"White, please, no sugar."

Last night, Paula had been at the pokies. She planned to go back there.

That horrible woman might be there. I'll go to another venue, maybe I will win another jackpot.

FORTY-THREE

Rodney
March 2008

THE GYM ROOM IS CROWDED, SWEATY BODIES PULL AT machines, handle weights, run on treadmills. The TV is always on. Paula pulls on the rowing machine with great effort. Groaning loudly. She has been coming to the local gym twice a week after work. Bored and drifting.

I miss Sarah so much. Wish I had the money to go to England and see her. There must be more to life than teaching, constructing research papers, and presenting at conferences.

She pulls hard at the rowing machine.

I am waiting for my life to begin. I used to be so focussed.

She showers, changes into her tracksuit and joggers. Goes home. Colin is watching the TV. He looks up when he sees her.

'When are we going to eat?" he said.

"Soon," she said through gritted teeth.

She slams cupboard doors, bangs pots on the stove, drops cutlery on the table.

"What's the matter with you?" he said.

"Nothing."

~

A month later, Paula presented a paper which was well received, at the Post-Traumatic Stress Disorder Conference held in Melbourne. It was there she met Rodney. They were seated next to each other at the conference dinner, had engaged in light banter during the meal. Rodney stated he was a lecturer teaching psychology at another building of her university. A vase of tall willow stems blocked the view of others at the round table. She had no recollection of anyone but Rodney that night.

Rodney noted her with interest. He recognized the emptiness in her eyes, understood the small behaviours and phrases that betrayed discontent. He noted the colour rising over her face as he bent close to speak to her.

Rodney had once been married to an agreeable woman who desired children, but he did not. In his own way, he glorified the women he slept with; sent funny cards, cheeky emails to maintain their interest. His speciality was married women, they made few demands and were grateful for any attention. If one of his conquests indicated a closer deeper relationship beyond sex, he became elusive, impossible to reach. Did not respond to phone calls, emails, was always very busy. It worked. They soon lost interest.

Rodney never pursued his students. They were too much trouble and, expected good grades for sleeping with him. He had experienced difficulties in removing himself from students in the past; they were sticky, hung around his office looking sad.

"Paula, your presentation on Post-Traumatic Stress Disorder intrigued me," he lied.

"I have an article that might interest you. We must meet to discuss your research further."

They exchanged phone numbers and email addresses. He proposed they meet at the university cafe 'to continue the discussion on the presentation.'

∾

A week after the conference, an email pinged in from Rodney.

"Let's continue the conversation tomorrow. Does 5 p.m. suit?" He said.

At 5.15 p.m., Paula arrived at the café. She was carrying the box of notes and handouts from the previous lecture.

"Sorry I'm late; it has been one of those days," she said, her voice bright, artificial.

"I thought you stood me up. Here, I have the research article I mentioned at the conference." His smile shows carefully capped teeth.

They order coffee, discuss the article, and agree to meet again. The coffee meetings morphed into regular lunch dates.

~

For the first time since Rachael died, Paula experimented with clothes, choosing bright colours. She tried a shorter haircut with highlights. Found herself humming. Looked forward to seeing Rodney again.

Colin noticed a change in Paula. "You seem relaxed these days."

Eventually Rodney convinced her to have sex with him. She is unsure. This side of life is foreign to her; has never cheated on Colin.

The sex happened in a humdrum motel not far from the university. He set the timer on his mobile phone as they undressed.

"Have to get back, meeting with my research students." He said, noticing her look.

Paula was aware the receptionist at the motel called him by his name.

Paula and Rodney developed a routine where they had sex every so often in the same dingy motel.

~

One day Paula entered a lift in Rodney's building at the university. She overheard two women discussing him.

"Rodney has a new plaything," said a full-breasted woman. She wore black spiky high heels.

"I wonder who she is. She doesn't work in the psychology department."

"Poor girl," said a blonde woman.

"Rodney sticks to his formula."

Paula does not look up, fiddles with her mobile phone.

"I pity any woman who attempts a serious relationship with him," said the full-breasted woman.

"I tried, you tried. At one stage, I even thought of leaving my husband for him. I must have been mad." The blonde woman laughs.

The lift door opens; the women hurry out.

How could I have become involved with a man like Rodney?

~

That night Paula arrived home early. Colin had finished his dinner of baked beans on toast.

"You told me you have late lectures on Tuesdays," he said.

"That has changed." She said.

She pours a double whisky, sips it. They sit in silence.

He hesitates to ask her what is wrong. Afraid of opening any touchy topic that may be circle towards Rachael.

"Well that's that," he said and folds the paper.

FORTY-FOUR

Rodney and the waitress
April 2008

RODNEY RAN HIS HANDS TO SMOOTH HIS CURLY BROWN hair. He leaned forward to speak to the blonde waitress. She smiled and nodded. He passed the waitress a napkin. She folded the napkin and placed it in her pocket. Grinned and ambled away.

Paula watched this interaction from the entrance to the café.

She sits next to Rodney. "Waiting long?"

"Every minute is an eternity until you come," he said.

She shows her teeth as if to smile. Speaks in a high-pitched tone, mentions the day's trivialities. Does not draw breath.

He puts his hand over hers. "Is everything all right?" he said.

She is silent for a few minutes, wondering whether to tell him or not.

"I heard two women discuss you. They intimated they both had a sexual relationship with you." Her face speckled with red blushes of embarrassment.

"What do you expect from a single man? I'm

not a monk," he said, voice indignant. "We're both adults." He holds her gaze. "I don't ask you about your husband." He drops his voice. "Perhaps you want to cool our friendship for a while."

Paula's mind flickers to a motor vehicle accident she passed earlier in the day on the way to the university. A thin man directed traffic around the accident. People hung out of their gardens, gaping.

A motionless body on the road, a helmet oozing bright blood, a motorbike on its side.

The sounds of an ambulance in the distance.

Life is so fleeting.

She remembers how bleak her life was before she met Rodney. How empty she felt. She knew her relationship with him was fleeting, wrong, felt deep guilt. Even anger. But for now, she could feel something.

It was better than being hollow. Is it better to have some measure of pleasure, or none?

"I'm famished, have you ordered?" she said. She breathed heavily. Removed her black tailored jacket, slipped it over the chair. The new blue silk shirt matched her eyes. The gold chain around her neck glistening. Her perfume followed her movements.

He watched her slow movements, beamed.

"I was waiting until you came to order," he said.

FORTY-FIVE

The memorial garden
May 2008

"KEEP DOWN, KEEP DOWN. HE'S STILL HERE,"

Rodney hisses to Paula, who had disappeared under the table at the restaurant.

The Carlton crowd is unperturbed, as if every day someone darts under a table. Paula holds her breathe.

A familiar brown trousered leg lingers near the table. Then after a few seconds the leg moves away.

What is Colin doing here?

"He's gone," said Rodney, peering under the table.

She scrambles up, smooths her skirt.

"I hate this."

"No law exists that says you can't have a meal with a colleague."

"I told him I was going to the Memorial Park."

"Lunch, Paula, we were only eating," he said.

"I should go."

"Coward," he said.

She looks up and down Lygon Street, no sign

of him. Locates her car parked in an underground car park.

Thumps the steering wheel.

What was Colin doing in Lygon Street and at that place?

She drives to the Memorial Park, parks near the curb. Unfastens the boot of the car, takes out a red milk crate and a cane basket. Locates the mildewed concrete seat. Steps along until she locates Row T. Finds the old bent gum tree in the centre. Counts twelve spots until she finds the right one.

It is freezing and overcast, a cold wind blowing. Small grey clouds scurry into each other and clump, creating a menacing wash in the sky. She places the red milk crate on the grass.

The bronze plaque reads:

'Rachael Wilson, 1989-2005

Dearly beloved daughter of Colin and Paula

Beloved sister of Sarah

Always in our hearts'

She lays out scissors, yellow polishing cloth, and bronze cleaner. Cleans and polishes the plaque, trims the small leaves of grass growing. Takes four pink Peony roses, places one in each corner. Everything must be perfect. Sits on the milk crate. Swallowed up by the surroundings.

Children are not supposed to die before their parents.

The pink Peony roses were Rachael's favourite. In another time, they planted the Peony roses together. Watered, added organic fertilizer, and pruned them. Removed the aphids by hand, squeezing between their fingers.

Rachael had wheeled the wheelbarrow filled with compost. Erected a blue plastic shelter around the roses to protect them from the frost. Paula has other roses in her garden. The Mr Lincoln rose with its blood-red colour and intoxicating perfume. The Just Joey rose with its orange blooms has a mesmerising scent. Rachael loved the Peony roses.

"They have cute curled petals and nice smell," Rachael said.

The Remembrance lawn is dry, the drought having been harsh. There are additional plaques every time she comes here. Next to Rachael's gleams a memorial for a child, Stephen, who died a year ago. She wonders if the mother is broken too. Stephens's plaque is perpetually glossy. There is evidence of recent polish and a decaying bunch of white daisies on the corner. She wonders about the significance of the daisies.

Half of Rachael's ashes are scattered at Indented Head, the rest here. She wanted to place the ashes next to the Peony roses at home. Colin refused.

"It would be too painful to know they were there," he said.

She sits motionless on milk crate. Whispers the Lord's Prayer. Clings to lessons learned from Sunday school. Thinks about an afterlife. Her words catch and swirl into the regions of the heavens.

Rachael my lovely girl, where are you?

Two magpies squabble in the bent gum tree nearby. They make their peace and fly off together. A tractor carrying a trailer chugs along the road, laden with five large rolls of ready lawn.

The wind rattles the trees. Leaves spring up alive, swirling around her, blowing in her face, brittle, dry, and brown. She wants to stop the burning pain inside of her.

The magpies fly back to the tree nearby. A car *swooshes* past.

Every month, Paula comes here hoping for closure. However, it has not come yet. Instead, grief suffocates until she cannot breathe.

Was there anything that I could have done to save Rachael?

The feelings are still raw.

Sometimes, Paula hears Rachael's laugh and turns but no one is there. She fingers the little plastic cat on her key ring. It belonged to Rachael.

"I have nine lives," Rachael said. She did not.

The wind builds, swirling leaves into circles nearby. Images of the past flitter by in her mind. Holding Rachael as tiny baby, kissing her delicate head, singing to her. Then the desperate prayers, contracts with an unseen God, "Let her live." The prayers answered came at a price. No one foresaw the brain injuries. Then the descent into heroin use, death.

I tried so hard to make a happy life for my daughters, but I failed.

She pulls at the gold chain around her neck, brings it to her lips.

Feelings hang in the air, as if closed in rooms covered with dust and mould. She opens the blue thermos. Pours a cup of hot coffee, nibbles on dry biscuits. Without warning, the rain starts. Paula throws the coffee onto the ground, picks up the milk crate and basket, and runs to the car. The rain stops as suddenly as it started. Raindrops slide on the windscreen.

Later she drives to the pokie venue opposite the Memorial Park, stays for an hour, loses $200. When she is in front of the machine, she forgets everything, the pain, the death, the ache.

On her return home, Colin said she had a double. He saw a woman who resembled Paula in Lygon Street.

"I was at the Memorial Park," she said, emptying the basket of remnants of flowers and bronze cleaner. She does not look at his face. The redness starts at her neck and spreads over her face.

FORTY-SIX

The research date
June 2008

PAULA GRIPS THE GLASS OF SODA WATER, HOLDS IT high above the throng of stomping dancers. Strobe lights flicker yellow, red, and blue, and flash over gyrating faces. The amplified bass reverberates through windows and floorboards.

"Paula," Rodney shouts, waving his arms, "Over here."

She edges through the mass of rhythmic bodies. His face turns red, green, and blue with the lights.

"Thanks for coming," he mouths. "We won't stay long." He holds a yellow legal pad in his hand filled with uneven scribbles. "Do you want to dance?"

"No," she said.

He grabs her hand. "Let's go outside." Collects his papers.

The noise of the throbbing beat seeps into the darkness.

"Is your project related to crazy music and deafness?" she said.

"A good topic but no," he said.

"Let's go to a motel and do our own research."

"And then?"

"You go back to your husband and I write up my notes."

"That's it?"

"That's it. Fabulous sex."

He beams at her. Hair flopped, shirt crumpled. He resembles a small child.

"What if I stay at your place tonight?" she said. Her eyes sparkle.

His face darkens a pause, and then he laughs.

"No joke," she said.

"Colin is away on business. I do not have to return home. I am free, I could stay with you. We could get to know each other. How about a movie? I could cook you something special. Give you a back rub." Her face earnest.

"Well," he hesitates to search for the right words.

"That is very nice." He clears his throat and pushes the hair out of his eyes.

"But my sister will be here for a few days."

"Your sister can stay in the spare room." Paula notices his uneasiness.

"She's old-fashioned." He looks away and tucks the shirt in his jeans. He takes a moment to speak.

"Actually, it's my ex-girlfriend coming."

"You told me you never see her anymore."

"Now and then."

"And she stays with you in your bed and you have sex?" she asks. Her eyes are wide.

"Paula…" he stops.

She shakes her head and walks to her car.

He does not call after her or try to stop her from leaving.

When she arrives home the phone is blinking, a missed message.

Colin's bright voice.

"Hello, sorry I missed you. I guess you and Jenny are out somewhere."

She looks at herself in the mirror.

You are an idiot, a stupid fool.

She pours a glass of whisky and water, sips it.

∼

Next day in class, Paula said to the students, "Don't forget the assignment due date. The assignment box will be cleared tomorrow at five. If your assignment is not in the box, you will register a failed grade. No extensions. The due date is the due date."

"That's unfair. I was hoping to get an extension," said one student.

"If you required an extension you should have requested it two weeks before the submission date. The university regulations are clear." She frowns at the student.

"Check your priorities and your motives for doing this course."

∼

Sarah sends a text message. "Hi, Mum, we will be away in London at the weekend. Maybe we can Skype the following weekend. Luv S xx."

Paula flicks the TV channels; so many advertisements for perfume and love.

FORTY-SEVEN

Jenny and Adriana
July 2008

FRIDAY NIGHT AT THE HOTEL, MEN AND WOMEN ARE cheek to jowl. Loud laughing explodes, background buzzes to the thump of drums.

"Paula's struggling," said Jenny, glancing at a thin man who is eyeing her from the bar.

"I'd hate to be in her shoes."

"She gives the impression she's doing fine," said Adriana. She flicked tiny strands of blonde hair from her face.

"No one could be okay under the circumstances," said Jenny. She pauses.

"When Rachael had PTA after the head injury, she was heavy going, shouting, and throwing things at people."

Stares at the man at the bar who holds a glass to her. Shakes her head at him.

"It takes a lot to rattle me, but I was out of my depth. God knows how Paula coped." She avoids the man's wave.

"No one can live with all that going on and stay intact," said Jenny.

Adriana was silent for a short while.

"Do you remember the time we had lunch at Williamstown at that café near the pier?" asked Adriana.

"I needed to go to the toilet and followed Paula to the loo. She appeared in deep conversation on her phone, didn't see me." She stops.

"Paula had her head to the phone like you talk to a boyfriend."

Adriana folded the serviette into four.

"A husband you hold the phone like this, head defiant. Paula cradled the phone close, oblivious to anyone."

"No." said Jenny's eyes wide.

"I overheard Paula say, 'Tuesday evening at the usual place,'" said Adriana.

"Then she looked up, saw me, and hung up. Just like that."

" 'Colin wanted to know what time I'd be home,' Paula said to me," said Adrianna.

"She looked flustered, guilty."

"Unfair," Jenny giggles,

"Soaking up my love life and keeping juicy secrets from us."

Jenny downs the last of the brandy.

"She's had a horrible life. Colin is as thick as a brick. I say good luck to her if she finds someone who makes her happy."

"I wish she'd stop pretending to be Paula Perfect."

Adriana rummages in her bag looking for a tissue.

"We could support her if she let us."

"Paula is a dear friend, but she has never confided much of a personal nature to me." Jenny is thoughtful.

"I met her mother several times. Now there was a monster. Her mother had a vicious streak. She berated Paula, even in front of me."

"Have you noticed how difficult it is to contact Paula these days? Her mobile goes straight to voicemail. It's often twenty-four hours before she responds," said Adriana.

"She's changed since the death of Rachael." She wipes her nose.

"She's built an impregnable wall around her emotions."

"I guess we have to be patient. This chap might make a difference."

FORTY-EIGHT

I love you forever and ever
July 2008

"I LOVE YOU," RODNEY SAID.

He rolls off her and kisses her on the nose.

The room has the strong pungent smell of sweat and musk. Wrinkled sheets and pillows pushed to the end of the bed.

"But do you love me forever and ever?" Paula's eyes bright.

"Forever and ever." He climbs out of bed.

The muscular body swaggers to the bathroom, He sings while showering.

"I love you forever and ever...and ever...and ever."

Lux soap and steam seep under the door.

She wraps the crumpled sheet around her naked body. There has been a change in their relationship. Rodney has been more attentive. Giving hints about making the relationship permanent. After years of Colin's impotence, sexual pleasure is a miracle.

She is lightheaded and giddy. Peers at the grimy ceiling. Notices the light bulb has no shade. Flowered wallpaper coming away at one edge.

"Are you going to shower?" he calls from the bathroom.

"In a minute..."

Rodney returns naked, dries in front of her. He jerks the white towel here and there, putting on a show. The guise of a man at ease with his world. Then dresses in blue Gazman underpants, white T-shirt, chambray shirt. Pulls his stomach to zip his jeans. He locates the brown loafers under the bed, slides on his leather bomber jacket.

"I am looking at one contented lady," he said.

She pretends to hide under the sheet, wraps it tighter around her. He unrolls her, exposing her naked body, lies on top of her.

"You are making it very difficult for me to leave. It will be your fault that my poor student must wait for me. There will be a complaint. I will tell them it is because of a certain sexy Paula Wilson."

He kisses Paula on the lips.

"I must rush. I love you forever and ever."

Then adds, "Same time next week?"

The door shuts with a metallic clang.

The afternoon light becomes orange and muted shades of brown.

Forever and ever, it sounds promising.

She showers, dresses. Looks both ways as she leaves the motel. The noise in Lygon Street is unnerving, locates her tram. It's packed with commuters. She holds onto the strap, has a remnant of a smile on her face.

~

"Oh, there you are." Colin comes running up when he hears her key.

"I am the bearer of good news." He beams with excitement.

"Step this way, my dear, step this way."

Two wine glasses sit in the middle of a platter of cheese and biscuits on the table.

"Your clever husband has won the contract."

"Well done," she said, raising the glass.

I wonder what Rodney is doing?

"I knew you'd be pleased."

He talks on and on, expounds on the complexities of getting the right bid.

"When the project is finished, we can go to England," he tells her. "The trip you always wanted. We'll see Sarah and Buzz and do a few tours." He dances around the room, holding the wine glass. "We need music," he turns on radio.

"It would be fantastic to see Sarah," she said.

~

Wednesday afternoon, Rodney phones Paula at work, "This is your forever and ever."

She laughs. "What are you doing?"

"I'm packing, going to Mildura, see Dad for three days."

"He will be pleased to see you."

"It will be over a year before I can connect again. My sabbatical leave came through. I am off to Oxford for a year." He mentions things on his list.

"Can't meet next week. Snowed under. Need to empty the office and pack. Find someone to take my cat." He pauses. "Do you want a cat?"

"No," she says.

She waits for the words: "Come to Oxford with me." They do not come. She is not part of his plans.

It caught her unaware.

This is how it ends.

Sharp, a knife stab to the chest.

She unplugs the memory device from the computer, shuts it.

Strides to the tram stop.

FORTY-NINE

A disturbing sight
July 2007

IT WAS ONE OF THOSE HORRIBLE DAYS. THE HEAD'S words churned in her ears.

"Paula, you haven't got what it takes to be a professor. I can't support your application for promotion."

Paula had sprinted from lectures and meetings all day. Each time she returned to her office, a gaggle of students waiting, demanding attention.

"I missed the lectures and need the handouts," or, "I can't think of a topic for the assignment."

It has been a long day...I can't wait for today to end.

~

Paula drove to the gambling venue after work.

I deserve a little time out.

Paula observed a disturbing sight. A furious young woman tried to drag an older woman away from a pokie machine.

"Time to go home while you're ahead," said the young woman.

"I'm on a lucky stretch."

"Come on. I'm going now," said the younger woman, throwing her bag over her shoulders.

"Give me a few more minutes." The older woman jabbed at the machine as the reels turned and stopped. Every so often, she banged on the screen three times, her lucky manoeuvre.

Five minutes later, the older woman turns to the young woman.

"Can you lend me $50?"

"No."

"Please? I'll pay you back when I get my pension."

"We're going home now."

"But I'm on a lucky streak."

"How come you lost your money if you're lucky?"

"You're so mean."

Paula keeps pushing the machine buttons, pretending not to hear. She watches as they leave.

"Fuck off," an abrasive male voice shouted next to Paula. He wore a blue bandana on his head.

A small brunette tugs his sleeve, her face beetroot red.

"Fuck off," he said.

"Mind your language," said a man on the other side of him.

"You can fuck off, too," his bandana slips.

He adjusts it with one hand, the other pushing buttons.

The brunette leaves.

Earlier Paula had lied to Colin, said she would be late home.

"I have a heap of photocopying to do before lectures tomorrow."

But she is at the venue again. In a trance slips a $50 in the slot.

Five more minutes.

Her money runs out. She contemplates raiding the parking meter stash of gold coins in her glove box. Decides against it. Drives home.

"You come home from work later and later," said Colin, a look of disapproval on his face.

She bangs saucepans. Drops the knife, then the fork. A plate slips from her hand and smashes into small pieces on the tiles. She cries as she sweeps up the mess.

"What's the matter with you?" he said.

"Get off my case. I've had a hard day," she said.

He pulls a face.

She is so edgy these days.

They eat in silence.

"Catalyst is on the TV," he said, getting up.

She cleans up, retreats to the office, checks emails. Makes a show of arranging the piles of student assignments. Sharpens a pencil. Cannot get started. Anger seeps through her body. When she's at the venue money is not currency, it's extra time on the machines.

How will I get the money back?

~

In the morning, remorse hangs around her. Her sleep has been fitful. The night terrors came; fear and dread woke her at 2 a.m. and did not let go.

Conscience came and danced on her chest and held a mirror to her face.

What if Colin finds out that I am gambling?

She felt miserable, unable to shield herself from self-hatred after the latest binge.

I am clueless and cannot overcome this gambling problem.

The chemical trajectory of the gambling had become a bright star, covered what was missing in other aspects of Paula's life. She had become hooked on the chemical high of gambling.

There is no sterner boss demanding satisfaction than a brain that arches up and demands the required burst of chemical.

Paula remembers reading an account of a man who had given up heroin for twenty years and by chance had driven though an old drug-using neighbourhood and had been so overwhelmed with the craving that he immediately stopped the car and scored. He started using heroin as before and slide into self-destruction.

She knew all these things in a way as you would know that the colour green is like grass but, it meant nothing if she could not do anything about it. She wondered if the chemical changes in the brain were permanent and always available to self-destruct.

My brain has changed. I have lost reason and intelligence.

FIFTY

The classroom
August 2008

"GAMBLERS BRING IT ON THEMSELVES," SAID THE caller on the radio. "Gambling is a sign of greedy, lazy people, wanting something for nothing."

The radio announcer interrupts, suggesting it might indicate depression or loneliness.

The caller crackles with laughter.

"Rubbish," she said.

"They're a lazy shiftless lot. I am tired of my taxes paying for people who are just too idle to get up and move on with their life, crying, 'Poor me.'"

Paula flicks the radio off.

Ignorant woman.

The car heater takes forever to warm. Paula shivers, tugs the collar of coat up around her ears. Drives to the university car park. Even at this early hour, a full sign is visible. She notices a smaller notice informing patrons renovations, no parking available today. Paula locates a spot in the street.

I must remember to feed the meter.

～

The classroom is an orchestra of chairs dragging and high-pitched voices. Concrete walls and wooden floors amplify the racket.

How can a tutorial class of twenty make so much noise?

"Presentations today. Please keep to the time limit."

Paula writes the names of the groups on the board.

I must remember to move my car.

Eventually, the final group. Two female students bound up. They have identical straight brown hair, which hangs to their waists. The shorter one shoehorned into very tight blue jeans. The other, tall and willowy, wears a cropped red jacket. They assemble the PowerPoint slides and collate notes.

"Our presentation topic is Problem Gamblers," starts the short one.

Paula shoots a glance from her marking sheet.

"I'll introduce the topic. Discuss statistics, theories, and elaborate on signs and symptoms." The short student nods to the tall student.

"My colleague will clarify treatment modalities."

"The Productivity Commission literature suggests that problem gambling is one of the most pressing problems for the Victorian Community," she said.

Paula perspires.

"I'm sure you know a problem gambler. The

medical issues are high blood pressure, migraines, stress-related disorders, cardiovascular."

She deliberates on gambling theories. Mentions intermittent reinforcement to hook people to keep playing the machines.

Paula's ears tingle. She feels vulnerable as though the students directed the presentation at her.

She half expects the student to add, "Even our lecturer today is a problem gambler."

The tall girl identifies current treatment modalities: Cognitive Behavioural Therapy, Gamblers Help Services, support groups such Gamblers Anonymous, and other treatments such as hypnosis. Pamphlets are distributed.

"Most problem gamblers originate from lower socio-economic groups. Those with mental health issues and those with addictions to alcohol and drugs."

Paula fumes, reviews the marking sheet.

Lower socio-economic levels indeed.

"Any questions or comments?" The tall student stares at the class.

A student at the back puts up her hand.

"My aunt developed a gambling problem after her marriage ended. She has a PhD in chemistry. The machines entrap vulnerable people," said the student.

A small smile spreads on Paula's face. She moves to the front of the class.

"Thank you for all of your excellent presentations today. Thank you, Roberta, for sharing your comments and reminding us that problem gambling is no respecter of economic status. We're all vulnerable to the effects of the machines."

The tutorial room empties. Paula wipes the white board.

"Are children of gamblers at risk to become addicted, too?" asked Roberta, holding a stack of folders.

"There's no conclusive literature related to genes and gambling," Paula said.

"Children do learn behaviours from their parents."

Paula continues cleaning the white board.

"I used to scream at her. It was my mother with the gambling problem," said Roberta.

Paula turns to the student, "Did your mother want to stop?"

"She tried many times. But she went back to the pokies whenever she was stressed," she said.

The student closed the door as she left.

Paula stopped.

I should stop gambling. I hate lying to Colin. Hate lying to myself.

The rubbish bins overflow with empty snack pack bags and drink containers.

~

Paula has always enjoyed teaching. She shares the students' enthusiasm to create a better world, to leave a mark and to fix social wrongs. However, some students are innocents.

"Why would a sane person stick a needle in their veins?" a student asked once.

Paula explained about pain and alienation. These notions were alien to those from protected well-off backgrounds.

Those who experienced the crushing despondency of dysfunctional lives understood.

Paula thought of one student who stood out from the others. She had black hair that swept to her waist. Wore expensive designer suits, had long red nails. The student spoke in a velvet voice. Gold bracelets jangled and clanked as she spoke. In Paula's office, the student disclosed she worked as an escort, servicing rich interstate executives. She planned to write a thesis on social support for sex workers.

∼

Paula checks her watch. Rushes to move her car. The parking officer is nowhere in sight.

FIFTY-ONE

Trying to connect
August 2008

"I HAVE TO TALK TO YOU," SAID PAULA. SHE HOLDS HER left wrist.

"Can't it wait?" Colin frowns, keeps typing.

She straightens a book from the bookshelf. It has come adrift from the neat rows. Flicks fluff off her cardigan. Searches for a tissue in her pocket.

It is always difficult to get his attention.

The phone rings. "Joseph. Did you get the quote I sent?" Colin's voice booms.

"Yes, I have time to talk, go ahead."

She shrugs her shoulders and moves to the kitchen. Polishes the clean sink. Arranges the newspapers in a neat pile. Gathers the dishes from the drainer and places them in the cupboard. Goes upstairs. Colin is still on the phone. She picks up her mobile.

"Hi, Jenny, can you talk?" she said.

"I was going to call you. Do you remember the long-haired chap at Adriana's party? We talked for ages, I thought we were on the same wavelength. I gave him my number. He rang just now, invited me to see the new French film tonight at the Nova."

Here we go again.

"I think I'm in love," says Jenny.

Paula sighs, recognizes the pattern. Jenny will heap fulsome praise on the man. Then, in four weeks, he is a jerk. Either married or otherwise committed. The ones who chase her and want to marry Jenny considers boring. She remembers Jenny had a trail of admirers panting after her at university. However, she hankered for the unattainable married professor.

Paula slips on her coat, strolls to the nearby park.

I wanted so much to talk to Colin about my gambling. To stop the lies and deceit.

FIFTY-TWO

Stopping
September 2008

SHE PICKS UP THE UMBRELLA AND OPENS IT. THE RED and white marigolds on the umbrella dance.

What am I doing? I am so jittery these days.

She replaces the umbrella in the stand.

Goes upstairs to the office. Rummages for scribble paper. Writes. 'Do not go to the venues and don't carry credit cards or money. Get counselling.'

She closes the door, is afraid her thoughts might filter to where Colin is watching football on the TV. She hates the door shut, quickly opens it. Breathes in the open space of the corridor, pushes the window open. Glances at the paper filled with scribbles, rips it into fours.

Walking might clear my mind.

She crosses the road, past the primary school. She finds herself in front of the venue as though an invisible string has pulled her.

Not today.

Crosses the street, past the funeral parlour and the African restaurant and the Housing Commission flats. The sky is shadowing. Decides to go back. The traffic has built up, cars snarl and snap at each other.

~

"Come, I want to show you something I found," Colin said when she returns.

She follows him into the garage.

"I found an old memory stick. It must have rolled under the bench." He plugs it in the computer.

"Do you remember Rachael's rock birthday party? I found a video clip." He puts his arms around her shoulders.

They watch the screen in silence. Images of the Rachael's party fills the screen, girls dancing and singing,

"I wish I had taken more video clips," he said.

She buries her face on his chest and cries.

"It is so hard to keep going. I want those happy times back."

"They were good times," he said holding her tight.

"I want them back so much too."

FIFTY-THREE

Played until the last dollar was gone
September 2008

THE DARKNESS WAS EVERYWHERE, ON THE ROAD outside and inside it was black. She was unsure of the time. But it must be morning as the trams had started running.

Another tram went past. Then quiet. It looked overcast, might rain.

She was trying to work out the unfathomable. Could see herself as a terrified young girl being pushed in the cupboard by her mother. The door locking, the darkness, the smell of mice droppings, mildew. Fear etched on the walls from the last time she had been punished here.

Somewhere a bird sang, she was not in the closed cupboard today but in another closed box, which was her life. No one would come to open the cupboard as her mother did years ago. Then she blinked into the light and saw the ordinary of the washing tubs and buckets. The copper in the corner. The windows open with the breeze blowing on the lace curtains.

No one came now. No one opened the box that was her life. She was captured.

She wondered if others felt this way, this emptiness, but of course never asked anyone for fear the facade would break and people would see her as she was, broken.

She looked at the prism of other lives. Wished she was like others, the ones she saw on trains and trams, the people laughing as she passed. Happy families. She watched friends and saw they were different families from hers.

A long time ago, Paula developed a way of seeing things or interpreting, not lying, pulling a tiny piece of truth and stretching it in a fashion that looked normal to others. Telling people unreal morsels that led others to think it was all OK.

"We had a picnic in the park," she said. Well the reality was she had taken herself to the park. And had drunk some water alone.

There was some truth there. Not a lie, a changing of the facts so they were palatable.

She learned the cues, memorised them, learned how to placate, learned how not to be harmed. That was an achievement.

The crazy part of her would arc up for no reason and she would go to the pokies and play until she had no money left, wasted, emptied her accounts.

Later the sane part would look at what she had

done and see that it was all madness. But at the time it was sense.

Secrets, she was a minefield of secrets.

∼

This morning Paula wondered if Gamblers Anonymous might offer motivation to help her stop gambling. She decided to attend a meeting.

The small, handwritten sign outside the wooden church hall stated: 'Gamblers Anonymous Meeting Wednesday 8pm.'

Paula waited in the car, observed a group of men and women drift in. A young man shook hands with the arrivals. He, too, disappeared into the building.

At 8:15, Paula crept in. She was fearful she might meet someone she knew. Located the small meeting room. Had hatched a plan to sit invisible at the back. To her dismay, men and women were in a circle facing a man speaking from behind a desk piled with books and pamphlets. She tiptoed to an empty seat.

Every eye turned to her.

The man next to Paula dabbed a handkerchief over his damp face and neck. A woman with thick glasses smiled at her.

Paula closed her eyes. Her heart raced.

Please, God, let it not be anyone from work.

A large Gamblers Anonymous banner hangs on the wall. The twelve steps embossed in gold.

Step one: We admit we are powerless over gambling, that our lives have become unmanageable.

Step two: Come to believe that a Power greater...

"That's the news on the picnic for now. Let's move to the main part of our meeting," the leader said.

The room reminded Paula of her Sunday school. Where she placed felt pictures of Jesus on a green board. The walls the same, dark panelled wood, gloomy. A long window high nears the ceiling.

The group read from the Gamblers Anonymous literature. The smiling woman handed Paula a copy. She pointed to where they are reading.

Paula read, "I gambled until my last dollar was gone."

I have done that.

The leader asked people to introduce themselves, use a Christian name, comment on the time of their gambling.

One woman said she has just come from the casino.

"So, it's hours I have not gambled."

Others mention specific months and years.

The sweating man reeked of beer.

"My name's Paula. Not gambled today." Her voice a whisper.

The words, once released, floated and clung to the wooden walls.

"Welcome Paula," said the group.

"Can someone share their story?" asked the man in charge.

A tall man in a tight navy suit and open necked shirt comes forward.

"My name's John. I'm a compulsive gambler." He said.

"Welcome John."

His narrative spoke of a long involvement with gambling: Pokies TAB, and sport betting. He mentioned wins at the beginning, then losses. Chased his loses trying to win his money back.

"Gambling changed my moral compass. I justified lies to gamble."

He took a deep breath.

"When I was young, I used to go to the TAB with my Dad. He taught me how to back a winner." He stops.

"I loved those times. It was wonderful to hear Dad shout with joy when he backed a winner." His face lights up.

"He used to buy me an Eskimo pie ice cream on the way back home after a win." He paused.

"We had to keep secret from Mum. She hated gambling of any sort. I wanted to be just like my Dad. I studied the form guide more than my lessons at school." His voice wavers.

"My gambling cost me my wife and children. I

stole from my employer to feed my habit until I ended up in jail for embezzlement." He wipes his face on a checked handkerchief.

"When in jail, I attended a Gamblers Anonymous group. Once I believed I had this gambling beat and stopped going to meetings. Before long, I was in trouble again. I never miss a meeting now. They remind me of who I am. To make sure I never get too big for my boots." He stopped and looked at the group.

"I haven't gambled for five years."

Next a thin middle-aged woman spoke.

"I used to go to the pokies after work with a girlfriend. At first, we had fun. Won a jackpot early on." She hesitated.

"Then I went by myself. Developed a heap of debt. Kept hoping for the big win to fix everything." Her hands shook.

"I told lies to my husband. Lied to the kids. Hated what I was doing. But I couldn't stop." She stared at the back.

"I gambled the kids' education money we had put aside, drew on our mortgage time and time again. My husband used to trust me with the finances." She clasps her hands.

"I tried to kill myself with pills. The kids came home from school and called an ambulance. I told my husband everything." Her face reddens.

"He gave me another chance. Does not trust me, even though I do not gamble, not even on a raffle ticket. He manages our money. My wages go into his account."

She removed her glasses, cleaned them with her skirt.

"I haven't gambled for two years and three weeks. If I'm late home from work, my husband assumes I'm at pokies," she said.

The group joins hands and recited the Gamblers Anonymous prayer.

Paula made a rush for the door.

A woman thrust a sheet of paper at Paula. "Here's a list of telephone numbers of people that can help you. My name is on the list. I am Maureen. Ring if you are tempted. I can help."

Paula shoves the list in her pocket.

I am not like these people. I can stop gambling anytime I wish.

The following Thursday Paula is at the pokies again. She plays until her last dollar was gone.

FIFTY-FOUR

A matter of life and death
September 2008

"Inheritance tax is up fifty-three percent," Colin said.

He studies the business section of *The Age* as others might a religious text.

"Mmm," she said.

The lamp light in the room cast a golden shadow.

They shared the hot summer's day at the beach. Bought battered fish and potato cakes and ate them, stretched out on the warm sand. Returned to the unit, opened a bottle of red wine.

Paula sensed a softness between them. She yearned to tell Colin she loves him. Beg his forgiveness.

He folded the newspaper.

"This is nice. We should get away more often," he said. His voice agreeable.

"Yes."

"You know," he stops.

"I wish things were different. I blame myself in

part for Rachael's death. I threw her out that day she stole money from my wallet." He hesitates, his voice lowers. "I felt I had no other choice."

She holds her head still. Places the book on the floor. Goes over to him. Kisses him on the forehead.

He holds her tight. "I'm not as strong as you."

She arches her eyebrows, drops her arms.

"I'd be lost without you," he said, his voice trails off to a whisper.

She said nothing, returned to her book.

~

That night in bed, she pats Colin's large belly spilling out of his pyjamas.

"Hey, watch it. That's my sexy spot. You could be in trouble touching me there. Or you used to be," he said. "We used to have good times in bed, didn't we?"

"Mmm," she said.

"One day there were two of us against the world. The world has ganged up on us since," he said. Colin watches Paula.

They tend to talk about neutral topics such as Sarah and her life in Cambridge. Now and then they touch on Rachael. She is a slippery crevice to fall in. The fall deep.

They mention mutual friends, trivia of the day. He stores up unusual things he hears on the radio and she relays quirky tales.

He stares at the door as though expecting someone to walk in. Now and then he will catch Paula miles away in thought.

"What's on your mind?"

Normally her response is light, trivial.

"The roses are nice this year," or, "We should invite so-and-so for a meal."

He never pursues it further, afraid to prod.

She comes home later and later from work. Has she a lover?

Paula's stares at the open pages of her book, not reading.

~

Paula is reliving Colin's heart attack. Even though it was years ago, every detail vivid. On a hot summer's day, like today, he slumped on the sand, holding his chest.

"You must get up now," she told him. "Soon it will be too late."

"The car is not far, we must hurry."

She tried to lift him. He was too heavy. He stayed on his knees in the sand, he looked like a small child praying clutched his chest.

"It's too late," he said in a whisper.

She remembered the seagulls, the waves on the beach, pulling back, crashing. The sky a brilliant yellow and orange. It had been hot.

"Colin, it's a matter of life and death. We must go now."

He clutched at her hand, tried to lift off his knees. He slipped in the soft sand. His left hand grabbed his chest. He stopped. The pain radiated up his left side.

She remembered that he fell face forward into the sand. Rolled him over pulled him up again. Recalled the yellow summer dress as it flapped around her legs, sticking to her. She searched the beach for signs of another human to assist. The beach deserted. She wanted run to the road and flag a motorist. She did not want to leave him.

Paula rummaged for her mobile, dialled 000. "Ambulance please, this is urgent."

"Indented Head Beach, near the pier. My husband is having a heart attack...Indented Head is between Portarlington and St Leonard's beach on the Esplanade."

The realization that the ambulance might not arrive in time knotted her gut. She reached for Colin's pulse.

"Thready...skin cold and clammy...pain in chest and shoulders."

"I love you," he said. His voice drowned out by the seagulls.

"The ambulance will be here soon," she lied. She remembered the fading light, the sky red. A small lamp on the pier came on. They clung to each other in the growing dark. His head slumped over her chest.

~

Tonight, he watches her expression, the book still open on her lap.

"Penny for your thoughts," he said.

"Oh, nothing much. We should have Jenny and her new boyfriend over for a meal. He's French."

FIFTY-FIVE

Silence
October 2008

Paula sat in the office, the room dark; she was enveloped in the dimness, not moving.

How could I have done it again?

She was full of self-loathing, needing to be punished, there was a part of her that was twisted, irrational, drove the rest of her. She wanted to scream, yell, tell someone of her pain.

Colin opened the front door and turned on the lights in the hallway. A glimmering light glowed the passageway. The rest of the house is in darkness.

"Paula?" he calls.

He knows she's home, saw her car in the carport. He climbs the stairs to the office and fumbles for the light switch.

"Don't turn—"

The light revealed Paula hunched on the floor.

"Switch it off," she said. Buries her face in her lap.

"Are you going to tell me what's going on?" He kneeled next to Paula.

She had her back against the green chair.

He moved closer to her, sensed her distress. Waited for her to speak. Is alarmed.

Something terrible must have happened.

Paula dragged herself off the floor. Colin followed her to the toilet. Waited outside. He can hear her crying. The toilet flushed, she came out. He watched her wash her hands, drying them finger by finger on the red hand towel. He has never seen her smudged and tear-stained.

She does not speak.

"What have I done?" He said.

He's waiting for the boom to drop.

"It is not about you." She strides into the kitchen.

They wait for the kettle to boil. She set out the cups, poured hot water over tea bags, squeezed the tea bags, placed them on the sink, and poured the milk.

She placed the two steaming cups on the table. After a time, spoke in a mechanical voice.

"I have a problem," she glanced at his worried face.

She cannot say the words, loses her nerve.

"Women's problems," she lied.

His face relaxes.

A menopausal thing. No one died. Sarah's fine.

He took two chocolate biscuits out of the glass jar. Offered her one. She shook her head.

"When are you going to the doctor?" he said.

"What?" She hesitated, confused, remembered what she said earlier.

"Next week."

Colin is out of his depth, is unsure what to say next. He hesitates, checks the clock on the wall.

"Time for the news."

She poured a full glass of red wine from the cask in the fridge, gulped it down. Washed the empty glass replaced it in the cupboard.

Turned on the hot plate. Pours a teaspoon of olive oil into the pan. Beat the eggs. Pours them into the hot frying pan. Makes a salad with tomato, lettuce, cucumber, and onion. Grates the tasty cheese. She sets out two plates, two sets of cutlery.

At 7:30, Colin returned to the kitchen.

"Would you like a glass of wine?"

She nodded.

He poured two glasses.

She placed the cheese in the middle of the omelette, folds it, cut the omelette in half, and placed equal portions on the two plates with the salad.

He mentioned snippets of news.

Paula has the sensation of hanging onto a rope slung between two ravines and the rope is shredding.

In five seconds, the rope will break, and she will fall into the raging torrent below.

FIFTY-SIX

Changes
October 2008

Sunday morning, Paula is wearing the old blue velour dressing gown. The sky outside is black. The only sound is the clicking of the computer mouse. She checks the social work students' assignment results. There is a nice bell curve with the right number of students passing, failing, and two-thirds under the curve.

She goes to the window, holding the cup of cold coffee.

The street is empty.

Could I have done more to help Rachael?

She made a promise to herself last week that she wouldn't go near the pokies. She wrote the date in her diary. Highlighted it with yellow.

There is movement in the lightening sky. A flock of birds fly past, roll, weave together as one, and disappear. Daylight tiptoes in without fanfare.

She remembers a poem called *Wholeness* by Pat Roeder-Thompson who wrote about gambling. "Give me back the pieces of me that I have scattered to the winds. Cutting, chipping gouging, left behind/with people, partners, places…"

How to get my old self back? Where to look for the pieces?

~

Later at the shopping centre, she decides on a massage.

A soft-spoken woman leads her upstairs. The walls are painted green, the staircase brown. White pebbles heaped in pots. The room is warm and scented with rose oil.

Paula undresses, slides under the dark green towel.

The woman massages Paula's back, neck and legs. She presses at tight muscles.

"Can you roll onto your front please?"

"I want to spend extra time on your shoulder muscles. They are very tight. You're harbouring negative energy there."

FIFTY-SEVEN

The sound of 100 machine guns firing
November 2008

EARLIER IN THE DAY JENNY, ADRIANA, AND PAULA MET for their regular lunch date. This time at the National Gallery of Victoria and to see the Oriental Exhibition. At the Tea Room, Adriana showed photos of her latest overseas cruise on the Rhine river with her husband.

Lucky Adriana married to a rich generous man.

The women hugged and said their goodbyes and, despite her best-laid intentions not to gamble, Paula is engrossed in the Dolphin machine at the venue near Flinders street railway station.

Thirty minutes until my train leaves.

Paula is excited, her eyes sparkle with anticipation.

Three drunk men shout to each other at the bar. Most patrons are staring at the pokie machines. Those sitting by the window comment on the darkening sky. The rain starts. A soft patter builds up in momentum and force, eventually grows in crescendo until it lashes at the windows. Yarra River disappears.

Boom and then the *rat tat* of a hundred machine guns firing. Hail unleashes its fury.

The patrons shout over the racket. A furious storm pounds the glass dome above the venue. Without warning, the dome smashes into a million pieces of glass on the panicked punters below. Men and women scatter to dodge the falling glass and hail from the broken dome. People bump into each other trying escape.

The yelling and screaming increases.

The noise is deafening.

The storm and hail create sinister layers of sound that terrifies the crowd.

"God save us, we're going to die," cries one woman. She crosses herself.

"Mother of God, help me."

The room quickly floods with rain from the broken dome. The carpet becomes a dangerous slippery lake.

How to get out?

Paula gathers her bag, ejects the money from the machine. She searches for the nearest exit. Edges towards the muted red light. In a flash of blue, the room lights up as lighting flashes. A boom of thunder follows.

"Take your money and go. It's not safe." Drenched venue attendants shout at patrons still playing on the machines.

Despite the commotion, one elderly man remains wedged to his seat. He hits the buttons repeatedly, ignoring the pleading of the attendants. Rain drips on his face. His glasses streaked. He refuses to budge.

"I'm winning," he says by way of explanation.

"If you stay, you'll be electrocuted. You must stop," said the attendant, his voice panicked.

"I'm not leaving."

Three security officers come over and haul the protesting man away.

"My winnings are in the machine," he cries.

"Your money's safe. You can collect it later. I'll put a reserved sigh over your machine."

"But I'm—" The thunder claps again.

Paula shivers.

She joins a group of sodden gamblers as they creep and slide towards the entrance. The venue is thrown into darkness. Patrons stagger and slip in the gloom. The air fills with profanities.

"I'll never play the pokies again," shouts one.

Paula reaches the exit and stares at the street.

It looks like the end of the world.

The storm has decimated the street. Cars, trams and buses stranded, shrouded with tree branches and hail. Flinders street glares white. It's still raining. Those waiting at the tram stop, attempt to protect their heads with newspapers and briefcases. Police sirens scream and are gridlocked in the non-moving traffic.

Paula clutches the soggy piece of leather that is her handbag. Her hair a wet mess, clothes saturated to her underwear, shoes squelch. She trails a group of men and women to Flinders Street railway station. No one checks the Myki cards. The passenger barriers deactivated.

Inside the railway station is the same chaos. Rain streams from the roof and glides from walls. The sound of hail and rain arches over panicky voices. The floor is treacherous here, too. Paula slips in a puddle of water, falls.

She locates a man in a Metro uniform.

"Are the trains running?" she shouts over the noise.

"No idea!" he yells. "You know as much I do."

Someone skids into Paula. The woman's packages spill out in the wet.

"Sorry," said the woman.

How could the fabric of order break down so quickly?

No one is in control. There are no announcements. No train information on the board.

Paula hovers in a corner watching others slip and fall on each other in the wet.

The rain rattles on the roof. People scream above the noise.

She rings Colin, he doesn't answer.

Paula edges to her platform.

The rail tracks covered in white.

Silent people stand.
An eerie hush.
How will I get home?

FIFTY-EIGHT

Email from Sarah to Mrs Gilbert
November 2008 Cambridge

DEAR MRS GILBERT,

Hello. A short email from Cambridge. I am happy here and can be my own person. The students are friendly, and I have made a heap of friends. Even have a boyfriend, his name is Buzz. We do the same subjects and study together. You would like Buzz. Your support in getting the scholarship was awesome. Thank you. I would not be here if you had not helped me. Thank you for telling me about your brother. It helped. Cheers, Sarah. P.S. My marks are high distinction and above.

FIFTY-NINE

Email from Mrs Gilbert to Sarah
November 2008 Melbourne

DEAR SARAH,

Your email made me so happy as I had been wondering how you are going. I am so pleased you are enjoying Cambridge and have a nice boyfriend. Please bring Buzz around to see me when you are back home. I appreciate you writing. I had worried that I overstepped my teacher's role when I spoke to you about my brother. Do you have many assignments? Are you enjoying the course? What have you seen of England? Please write again. Kind regards, Dorothy Gilbert

SIXTY

Email Sarah to Jenny
November 2008 Cambridge

HELLO JENNY,

I love it here at Uni. The parties have been awesome. Friday nights, we go to the pub and get wasted. My boyfriend Buzz said he wants to meet you. I told him how much fun you are. I cannot believe you and mother are friends. You are both so different. Mother sends me nagging notes about studying hard and always mentions Rachael. Dad writes funny emails. Write please. Love, Sarah xx

SIXTY-ONE

Email Jenny to Sarah
November 2008 Melbourne

DEAR SARAH,

Wow. A nice boyfriend. I wish I could find someone special. Glad you are enjoying life and kicking up your heels. Your mother was not always straight-laced. I should tell you the hijinks Adriana, your mother, and I got up to when we were at university. She was a different person then. Life has changed her. I want to see photos of Buzz and you. I am still going to jazz dancing but it's not as much fun without you. Miss you darling. Hugs and more hugs. Love, Jenny xxx

SIXTY-TWO

After the hail storm
December 2008

Paula takes a sip of the chilled water at The
Indian Star restaurant. Soft Indian music enhances
the harmonious setting. Colourful tapestries
depicting scenes of marriage ceremonies hang on
the walls. Tasteful artefacts placed on the floor.
Wooden musical instruments lay on a stand. The
restaurant fills with cheerful families. Couples
hold hands.

Paula looks at her watch. It is dark outside,
Jenny is half an hour late.

*It will be good to see Jenny and have a laugh. I
wonder why Colin rang from his business trip.*

"Jenny and I are planning to eat at The Indian
Star," she said to Colin earlier.

"We may go back to Jenny's. She wants to show
me her Paris photos."

"Don't be late home; I worry about you," he said.

Paula has been reliving the hailstorm. Thinking
of the old man's reluctance to leave the pokie
machine even with rain pouring over him from the

broken dome. He had put his life in danger, could have been electrocuted.

Did he go back to collect his money?

Her phone rings. It is Jenny, full of apologises.

"Just parking the car. Be there in five minutes. I have such a story to tell you."

Jenny soon blusters in full of apologises.

"Sorry, I'm the worst friend in the world," She gives Paula a hug.

"Are you angry with me?"

"Who have you fallen in love with today?" Said Paula.

"This is a most amazing story." Jenny's face is radiant with pleasure.

"You will never believe it. But I ran into Bob again." She takes a sip of water.

"There I was waiting in the queue at the bank. And he was in front of me. I said hello. He said I was still as gorgeous as ever." She grins.

"By the time we were at the counter, we made a date to meet." Jenny giggles.

"Wasn't he married?" asked Paula.

"He's divorcing his wife." Her voice betraying annoyance.

"I'm starving, let's order." She looks up at Paula.

"Did I tell you I received an email from Sarah? She has a boyfriend. He sounds nice," said Jenny.

"I hope she's studying as well," said Paula.

"Don't be grumpy. We should fly over and surprise Sarah during semester break."

"We should," said Paula.

Where would I find the money to travel overseas?

"Are you ready to order?" Said the waiter.

At 10:30, go their separate ways.

Paula does not go to the pokies as she had planned, instead drives home.

The old man at the pokies, Jenny and I are the same. We hang onto to foolish hope.

SIXTY-THREE

It feels like a lucky day
January 2009

IT IS 5 A.M. MONDAY. PAULA IS MOTIONLESS ON THE green armchair. She holds a cup of coffee with both hands. Her hair matted. The cord from the navy velvet dressing gown hangs. She has goose bumps over her body. Bach's St Matthew's Passion plays on the laptop computer. A faint smell of Arpege perfume lingers.

The contents of Paula's handbag are upended on her desk. Diary, pen, address book, keys, mobile phone, lipstick, compact, small bottle of Arpege perfume, three tissues, a purse with no money. Four crumpled receipts piled to the side. She puts down her cup. Again, counts the receipts.

$100, plus $200, plus $200, makes $500, and $200, is $700. No, that cannot be right, it can't be $700.

She fingers the wedding and engagement rings on her fingers, slips them back and forth. Counts the ATM withdrawals again. Holds her head. The $700 ATM withdrawals occurred in the space of three hours Sunday. She rips them into hundreds of pieces until they resemble black-and-white confetti.

I couldn't have gone to the ATM four times. There must be an explanation, a bank malfunction, a mistake.

She tightens the dressing gown cord around her waist, pulls it too tight. Paula opens the drawer of her desk. Takes out a small pair of scissors and with furious strokes chops up the Visa card into four squares. Cuts repeatedly until only thin slithers of blue plastic remain. Dumps them in the bin. She is dazed, unsure what to do next. Replaces the contents of her handbag. Her heart pounds. She gasps. Sees another ATM receipt, half-embedded in the address book. She checks the receipt, $200 Sunday.

Oh, no, $900 dollars.

A wave of nausea comes over her. She places a hand over her mouth, wants to vomit. Paces back and forth in the room, is a caged animal looking for a way out.

Beats her fists on her head trying to feel something.

Digs nails deep into her hands leaving indentations.

Bites her bottom lip.

Thinks of a colleague who had committed suicide.

What is happening to me? How could I have blocked out the five trips to the ATM. It is like the gambling has taken hold of my brain and I do not know who I am anymore.

~

In the previous weeks, she has tried hard to connect with her old self. She attended yoga classes, meditated, swam.

~

Sunday, it started with a whisper, a tiny, single shining thought floated and murmured, caressing. She finished pegging the week's washing, assorted his and her shirts, slacks, underwear, towels, sheets. She watched the clothes flapping on the clothesline. Paula carried the empty clothesbasket, stepping up the back steps to the laundry. She mopped the floor. A thought gathered momentum.

It feels like a lucky day.

She changed into the black tracksuit with the white stripe, zipped the hooded top, pulled on sneakers. Paula extracted the Visa card from its hiding space in the bottom drawer of her desk under the folder of notes for lectures.

$100 will be the absolute limit.

The whine of the router established Colin working in the garage, cutting and breaking timber. Paula stood at the entrance, the small particles of pine fibres created a brown storm. Every surface covered with debris, hair, safety goggles. He stopped the router and removed his earmuffs and goggles.

"I'm going to the gym," she said. She swung the gym bag. "I'll make lunch when I get back."

Colin nodded, replaced the goggles and earmuffs.

She never made it to the gym. Drove to the pokie venue.

～

Today, she recalls a medical journal article that suggested electronic gaming machines affect the same part of the brain as crack cocaine. Paula's gambling had become the one true thing in her life. Each machine had its own music that coaxed and petted her. The cheerful noises, the screen lighting up with words of praise.

"Well done. Congratulations."

The pokies were the fire and colour of her day, lifting her, raising her out of the darkness and opening to possibilities.

It was the one place on earth that did not remind her of Rachael.

SIXTY-FOUR

Jenny's lunch
February 2009

THE WOMAN RUBS THE HAIRY CHEST OF THE WELSH corgi.

"So, you've come back to check on me, Dino."

He stands on the tips of his paws, looking at her face, licks her hands as she gives him a pat. His dog face opens into two parts, a red tongue pants to one side. The dog smells of mowed grass, coat dusty and covered in twigs and leaves where he has rolled.

The dog runs in tight, ever-decreasing circles chasing his tail, a flash of exuberance in tan, a brown rocket shooting through the park. Chases birds flying low, announces himself to children on bicycles. Follows mothers with prams.

Children plead to pat the doggie.

Dino skids to a halt near a girl on the swing, circles, barking encouragement.

As if by elastic, he bounds back to the old woman on the bench, saliva dripping from his mouth, face ecstatic, panting at her feet.

She ruffles his chest fur. "You're a clever dog,"

He leaps into the air and sprints again, fat dog feet creating a tunnel of leaves behind him.

"Dino is very spoiled," she said, turning to Paula who is seated next to her on the park bench.

Paula is in no mood for chat with strangers. She turns her back, hoping to shut the woman out.

The dog is a nuisance. Where is his leash?

Paula's thoughts are on the luncheon earlier. Anger whirls around and creates its own knot of self-righteousness.

Blast Jenny, she is so inconsiderate.

~

Earlier in the day, Paula vacuumed, mopped, prepared Chicken Kiev and roast vegetables, tossed a green salad, and made chocolate cheesecake. The coffee perked, wine chilled, the kitchen breathed chicken. Beethoven played in the background. She picked three perfect pink Peony roses from Rachael's rose bush. They sat beaming at the table. Paula checked herself in the glass of the oven.

She adjusted the black V-necked jumper pulled over blue jeans. Lit the small candle under the oil burner and placed three drops of orange essence into the water. The room fills with orange, warm, and inviting.

The kitchen of pine wood cupboards and white benches gleam. Saki plates and matching dessert plates on the bench. Coffee cups and saucers on the silver tray. Sugared almond biscuits perch on a tiny dish.

At 1 p.m. the doorbell rang. Jenny bounced inside.

"Hello, something smells nice. Put this bottle of white in the fridge; it needs chilling." She nodded to the stranger standing behind her.

"Linley invited herself to our luncheon." She smiled nervously.

Paula stared at the tall, manicured, blonde-haired Linley person at her door. The woman had a granite face, long swinging earrings.

"I hope you don't mind. I begged Jenny to let me tag along." Linley's American accent emphasised by Chanel No 5.

Paula opened her mouth; no words came out.

"What a sweet little home, Paula. May I look around?"

Linley clattered around the house, opening doors.

"Sorry. I should have warned you. Linley pounced on me as I was getting in my car," Jenny said.

"I only have two Chicken Kievs," Paula said, a scowl on her face.

"She can have half of mine."

"Is that your garden?" Linley peered out of the kitchen window. The garden a mass of red and pink roses.

"What a sweet little garden."

"Are you all right? I'll ring tonight, and we can talk," said Jenny.

Things were not all right. The credit card debt had blown out. Colin suspected something. Paula felt as though she had swum out to the deep end of the ocean and lost her energy to swim back.

"Your kitchen cupboards are so seventies. I have a white kitchen. In fact, white everywhere," said Linley. "I live in a large apartment," she said waving her arms. "Overlooking Central Park in New York. I can see the whole world. At night, the lights are fantastic."

Paula's eyes narrow.

What an ignorant woman. Who did you think you are? Coming in uninvited to my home and criticising my décor.

"I'll move this vase from the table. It's in the way," said Linley. She places the vase with the Peony roses on the sink. "You don't mind if I smoke, do you?" She lit a cigarette. "I can use this saucer for an ashtray," she said, blowing smoke in the kitchen.

"This is a non-smoking house," said Paula through clenched teeth.

"Just one cigarette," Linley said.

Paula screwed her face and waved her hands at the smoke.

"Please stop smoking, I hate it."

"Oh dear, I made you cross," said Linley in a

little girl voice. She extinguished the cigarette in the saucer.

Paula glared at Jenny, who avoided her glance.

At lunch, Linley shared her perceptions of the Social Work conference.

"It was mediocre," she said.

"The conference participants didn't understand my social work model of care. Addictive behaviour reflects adolescent uncoupling from a demanding mother."

Linley is a fool, thought Paula.

"Australia is behind the rest of the world in social work theory," said Linley airily.

Jenny caught Paula's eye and winked.

"I'm going to the casino tonight. Jenny is going to take me."

"Come with us," said Jenny.

"No thanks, I have a stack of papers to mark," Paula said.

The lunch was soon over, after they left, she blew the candle under the oil burner, opened the window to eradicate Chanel No 5. Replaced the vase of pink Peony roses to the centre of the table. Stacked the dishes in the sink. Pulled the black coat from the hall stand and headed to the adjacent park.

∾

Back at the park, the old woman on the bench is still talking.

"Ben was no trouble, even when he developed dementia. I'd bring a thermos of tea and biscuits and we'd have a picnic when it was warm," she said.

"If he could see me, he was content. But in the end, he forgot who I was."

She drops her voice, then regains her composure.

"He had no memory of anyone. He was a wonderful husband." She looks at Paula.

"We were married for sixty years."

The woman had silvery hair, curled into a tight white bun at the back of her head. She rolls her hands under the fur collar. Adjusts the red silk scarf tied around her neck.

"I never expected Ben to die before me." She turns her head towards Dino.

"My sister Mavis bought Dino for me."

"He is an active little dog," Paula said.

After one last running jumping marathon, Dino collapsed at the woman's feet.

"Are you done?" She strokes his heaving white chest.

"I have a married son who lives in London. They have a daughter named Elsie. My son keeps asking me to come and stay. But if I do, what will happen to Dino?"

The woman's face creases.

She clips the leash.

The woman touches the sleeve of Paula's black coat. "Thank you for listening to an old woman's ramblings" she said.

She walked away the dog trotting alongside. "You had a glorious run today," she said to the dog.

Paula doesn't move. She can't imagine any marriage surviving for sixty years, not hers anyway, pulls her coat tight.

The silent gum trees stand tall together.

Paula watches the lights come on in the houses. Imagines fathers coming home from work, hanging up coats, greeted by ecstatic children clinging to their legs. Wives with aprons kissing tired faces.

How can I tell Colin my credit card debt is $20,000? He'll go ballistic.

She can imagine the shouting. Money was a measure of his manhood. Money to her was time at the pokies. Checks the time, 6 p.m.

A great whispering wind rises in the park swirling and moaning, pushing leaves into small circles. A flock of galahs appear, colouring the sky pink.

Paula stomps on Dino's pile of leaves. Scuffing her feet this way and that, gaining momentum, kicking harder and harder until she's exhausted.

A man jogging makes a wide arc to avoid her. The dark settles. Paula digs deep in the pockets of her coat. Exhausted, she stops, walks home.

～

"How was your lunch with Jenny?" Colin asks.

"She brought a friend along."

His face is glued to the news. Another bomb has exploded in Iraq killing forty people. A bridge collapsed in Turkey drowning ten cars who fell into the river. A train crash in China kills 250.

Where is the joy of life? Everything is darkness.

"Is pasta okay for tea?" Paula said.

He nods.

Paula fills a pot, browns meat, onions, and peppers. She adds garlic, and oregano, opens a jar of sauce. Makes a salad. She pours the remains of the Hardy wine, sets a tray. When the water boils, she throws in the pasta. Sets the food on a plate and gives it to Colin.

"Smells good," he said.

"Where's yours?"

"I had a big lunch."

She does the dishes and climbs the stairs to the study.

Commences marking the pile of assignments.

At 11 p.m. he comes to kiss her goodnight. "Don't stay up too late."

"I won't."

She listens to his footsteps in the hall. The toilet flushes, teeth brushed, then silence.

I don't know myself anymore.

SIXTY-FIVE

Dino dies
March 2009

PAULA STRIDES HOME FROM THE TRAM STOP TO Westbourne road. It has been a good day. She submitted an article for the *Social Work Journal*. Completed the data analysis for the project related to homelessness and trauma. Most students in her research class handed in their proposals on time. Overall all her classes went well. The irritating students who normally text far-away friends were involved in the class.

Without warning, a blur of a dog darts out on the road followed by a squeal of brakes and a nauseating *thud*.

A young man bounds out of the Holden Commodore. At the front tyre lays a still brown and white Corgi. Blood seeping from his head.

"Dino...Dino..." The woman rushes to the dog. She kneels next to him.

"My dear little friend." She touches him.

"He ran in front of me, I didn't see him." The young driver shouts, his face panicked. I would never have hit him on purpose, I love dogs…" He covers his face.

"I killed a little dog," he said to himself. Turns to the woman, tears running down his face.

"I am so sorry."

"It's my fault. I let him off the leash," she said.

"I never killed anything in my life" he said.

Paula grips her briefcase. She wants to go over to comfort the woman. But cannot move. She remembers the woman from their conversation in the park. Tightness spreads across her chest.

Did Rachael get hurt like this? Was she thrown over a windscreen?

She wants to be vomit, run away from the place.

It is too raw and the thought of her daughter lying on the side of the road like the little dog is too vivid.

Dashes home, struggles to fit the key in the lock.

Colin finds her sitting on the divan, still clutching her brief case, the handbag flung over her shoulder.

"You look dreadful. What's happened?"

"There's been an accident. Someone died." The words hesitant.

"Who died?" His voice full of concern. Sits down beside Paula.

"A dog died. I saw everything. It was horrible." She pauses. "I ran home." Drops her head.

Her words muddle, as if in a stream of

consciousness, rambles about the effect of seeing a small dog, lifeless on the road.

Her hands shake as she tells the story.

Blows her nose on a crumpled tissue.

Turns to look at Colin.

"Someone helped Rachael when she came off her bike and stayed with her. I didn't help anyone today."

"There are things you don't know," her voice hoarse.

Silence hangs in the room.

He waits for her to speak. He had been dreading this moment.

"You've had a shock. I'll make a cup of tea."

"There is so much about me you do not know..."

She grabs his arm, holding him.

Sentences run into each other.

She tells a horror story.

Doris locking her in a cupboard.

Beatings as a child. Fear of her mother.

He grimaces in disbelief but listens without interruption.

"I'm still locked in," she said.

"I can't get over Rachael's death. No matter what I do, I am not coping."

She jumps from one topic to another.

It's impossible to follow.

"You did your best. We did. It was uncharted territory for us." He holds her hand.

"I'm a hypocrite. Pretend to help people. Just

now I did nothing to help the woman with the dog." She stops.

"You think I'm mad." She looks at him.

"I failed Rachael."

"Don't be ridiculous, you were the only one who never gave up on her. You did everything above and beyond." He said.

"I was ashamed of Rachael's heroin use," she said, looking in the distance.

"I wanted to change her to make me better." She jabs at her chest.

"After Rachael died, I was crazy with grief. I blamed myself.

And," she says in a small voice, "I've been playing the pokies after work. It helped me not to feel. It stopped me going mad."

He drops her hand.

"I've maxed out two credit cards." Her face scarlet.

He does not speak, is cold, unflinching. Clears his throat.

"How much money do you owe on the cards?"

"Near $20,000 dollars," Her face crumpled, tear stained, leans towards him.

He pulls away. Shakes his head, whistles. Tries to digest the amount.

"$20,000. My God that is a year's salary for some people. How long did you spend at the pokies?" He looks away.

"So, you must have been lying to me all those

times you said you were working late. Instead, you were at a gambling venue losing money on the pokies." He stared at her.

"You lied to me." His voice loud like a clap of thunder.

His face hard like stone, fists balling up by his side.

Gets up puts his hands in his pockets. Then takes them out, cracks the knuckles.

"What do you mean about $20,000? Is there more?" His voice now has a knife edge.

"You must see the bank, get a loan to pay the cards. Get help." Colin stares unblinking

"I'm working my guts out and you are throwing money on the pokies. No way am I bailing you out." He stops, fury written on his face.

"Look at you; you are not even sorry. Well, you got yourself into this mess and you can get yourself out. So much for your fine academic degrees and educated friends."

He leaves the room in disgust

"Colin, please." She wants him to hold her, say that he loves her no matter what. The two of them could work this out.

Paula knew when she saw his face that it was a mistake to tell him.

Now there will be nasty repercussions.

He couldn't or wouldn't see her grief and that it led her to gamble.

The snake pit is my life.

SIXTY-SIX

The stranger
April 2009

It's been a month since Dino died. She promised Colin she would not gamble again. And meant it at the time. But work has been very stressful. And finds small comfort in the escape of the machines.

She feels guilty.

The last two weeks she has slipped up a few times and against her better judgement has gambled after work.

Paula never made it to the bank to cancel the credit cards. Instead, organized replacement credit cards for the ones she cut up earlier. She manages to pay only the minimum payment on both cards.

Although she knows it is stupid, both as a health professional and common sense, she fantasises of a big win to clear the debts.

One part of her brain, the sensible part, tells her *Stop*.

The other part of her brain that is used to the chemical high of the pokies and wants more, hijacks good intentions and suggests *Just a few minutes*.

Paula hates being deceitful to Colin and is conflicted. But sees her gambling as a release from her stresses, a safety raft.

∿

"I know where you live." A stranger reeking of beer with a toothy, sardonic smile, taps her shoulder.

Paula is gambling at the local venue, in a mind bubble, a zone.

Paula gasps, surprised, pulls back, shaken, drops the coin cup.

The coins clatter as they fall to the ground.

She stares up at the man up at the man.

Panic rising in her chest.

"Does Colin know you're playing the pokies?" the man asks. His voice conspiratorial. He winks.

A strong heavy hand grips her shoulder. His wrinkled face close to Paula's.

"Who are you, what do you want?" her voice panicked.

She glances at the woman playing next to her. Hoping for help. The other woman is oblivious to anything beyond her machine.

"Go away. I'll call security," shouted Paula.

The stranger makes a nasty mocking laugh. "Call away," he said and gives a malicious grin.

Then as suddenly as he came, he disappears, melts into the crowd of men at the bar.

Who is this idiot? How does he know Colin?

She kneels, collects the coins scattered on the ground. Her heart beats wild and fast. Flings the coins into her hand bag. Glances around for the stranger who is still at the bar.

She grabs her black coat from the back of her stool. Strolls out, head held high.

Paula makes a detour away from the bar to the exit.

The coins make a clattering noise as she walks.

Once out of the venue, makes a dash to the nearby car park. Locks the doors in her car. She peers in the rear vision mirror. Her heart jumps.

The stranger stands illuminated under the lights at the entrance; he waves.

Who is this horrible man? Who is he and how does know Colin? Is he a psychotic killer going to murder me?

The short drive home is torturous. Sweat drips down her face, hands slip from the steering wheel. Her heart beats a thousand beats a minute. She can barely breathe.

She keeps turning her head to check the rear-view mirror.

No one is following.

Paula runs into the house, deadlocks the door. She pulls the curtains across and opens them a chink and glances at the street. No one there.

Just a drunk.

"What are you doing?" asked Colin watching her.

"A stranger frightened me tonight," she said. Her breathe coming in bursts.

"Whoa," he said.

"Start from the beginning."

She tells him the story of the stranger. Alludes to seeing him in the supermarket.

"What did you buy? Where are the shopping bags?" His voice hard like a rock, unsmiling.

What's the connection with the stranger who might want to hurt me and shopping bags?

Colin's face cannot be read.

"I intend to report the incident to the police," she said, reaching for her mobile phone.

"Don't," he tells her. Puts a hand over hers.

An icy draught fills the room.

In her mind, Paula is six years old again, her mother blocking escape. Doris grabbing her with one hand and slapping her with the other.

"I don't understand." She stares at his large hand still gripped on her hand.

"A stranger frightened me. He may have planned to harm me. Why are you telling me to back off?" She pauses. After an eternity, the brain clicks.

"Do you know this man?" She asked in a small voice.

No one speaks.

He releases her hand.

"A friend of mine has been shadowing you," he said. "I've had my suspicions you've been up to something."

"My God," she said, developing insight into what was going on.

"Did your friend tell you where I was?"

"You weren't shopping."

The refrigerator whirls.

Colin spoke, "Where do you get the money for the pokies? I remember you told me you were going to cancel your credit cards." His voice tight. They had a bloodied edge to them.

"Tonight, was my first night in ages," she said.

Her mind scrambling to find a plausible excuse, a way out. She feels faint, cornered.

"My friend tells me you have been at the venue twice this week."

She places both her hands on her head.

"I thought you might be gambling again." He glares at her. "I ask again, where do you get the money to gamble?"

"I used my tax return," she lies. She had not seen this coming.

"I tried to stop." Her face scarlet.

"It looks that way, doesn't it? How to stop gambling by going to the pokies." His voice threatens.

"Paula, the clever academic." He spits the words out. "You discovered the solution to gambling addiction. Play the pokies more and lie to your husband. I wonder if it works for alcoholics, too." He stops. "When we had our talk last month, I believed you. Gave you a chance. But it seems you prefer time with a stupid machine than spending it here with me." His face is etched in pain. "What else is lies?"

Paula has difficulty understanding. Bolted to the floor. Trembles.

Frozen unable to speak.

You disgust me, Paula. I'm not sure I want stay married to you."

"I'll go for counselling, I promise." She is pleading.

Colin shrugs his shoulders, shakes his head and disappears up the stairs.

I can't believe it. He had someone shadow me.

SIXTY-SEVEN

The credit card
May 2009

WEEKS PASS, PAULA DOES NOT RETURN TO HER USUAL pokie venue. She comes home early most days and they eat together. Colin and Paula share stories of their day as before. Everything appears normal on the surface, but everything has changed. There is a façade of politeness. Underneath is bitterness and resentment.

She cannot get over the thought of Colin had her followed.

And he cannot come to grips with her gambling and wasting money. What galls him the most are her lies. He does not believe anything she says now.

One day, after a particularly horrible interaction with the nasty Head of School, she escapes to a venue to play the pokies. Paula is engrossed in the playing and winning and losing that does not realise how late it is.

She tries to think of a plausible excuse to give Colin.

What shall I say? I had a meeting...no, too late.

Photocopying handouts for students... That might work...I hate telling fibs but to tell the truth would have terrible consequences for me.

The street is in shadow. She edges the car into its spot under car port. Sits gripping the steering wheel. The windscreen fogs. She gets out, collects the briefcase, and swings the handbag over her shoulder. Quietly turns the key and instantly knows she's in trouble.

The television is blaring, half the house in darkness.

As soon as he hears the key, Colin switches on the lounge room light.

She jumps in fright.

"Queen Paula, I see you have graced me with your presence." He's scowling, clutches a Foster's stubby. "You remembered at last where you live. Do you know the time?" He holds up his arm and points to his watch. "The big hand is on six and the little one on nine. That makes it 9:30 at night. I am sure you have a good excuse? Were you lost? Working so hard you forgot to come home?"

Her eyes darken. "I was at the university, preparing handouts for the students—"

"At the university." He laughs a horrible laugh. "Don't give me that balderdash, Paula. I called your office at least four times tonight. You were not there. You'll find four messages rising in panic and volume on your answering machine when you go to work tomorrow. Don't tell me you were photocopying until 9:30 p.m."

She opens her mouth to speak, but nothing comes out. Her face guilty, flustered, cornered.

I wish the earth would open and swallow me.

"So, where were you? Remember me, I am the husband." He thumps the stubby to his chest.

"I'm not as smart as your university friends, but I pay most of the bills for this household." His voice expands in volume. He throws his arms around, spilling beer over the carpet.

Paula is about to say, "Watch out," but says nothing.

The peach-coloured carpet is spotted with beer stains. He sees her looking and drips beer, taking pleasure at the shock on her face.

"After I photocopied the handouts, I had a coffee with a colleague at the university," she said.

"First it was work and now it's coffee with a friend. Which friend and where did you go? I will give them a quick ring and verify your account.

The television blares.

Paula puts a hand to her head, "Can you turn that off?"

He mutes the TV. Images of football players in striped uniforms kicking and falling create a blue wash in the room.

"Paula," He moves close to her face. "I had an engaging phone call today from the bank." His breath reeks of beer.

"The bank?"

"Yes, the bank. The bank manager at the ANZ was pleased to inform us that our application for an extension on your credit card limit is confirmed. Do you want to tell me more? Remember our honest little chat last month when you said you were cancelling your credit card account.? From cancelling your credit card, you extended the limit." His face monstrous. "Are you gambling again?" He looks right in her eyes.

The old fear sends her into a trance, unable to speak, unable to answer.

Anything I say will inflame him further.

"I work my guts out, so you can piss our money up against the wall," he said.

"I only gamble with my money," she said, her voice a whisper.

"Oh yes, I forgot. It's your money. While you feed the pokies. I am paying the bills.

Electricity, gas, rates, insurance, wireless connection...I won't go on. You know what I mean. Is this fair? Does that sound right, Paula?" He stares at her.

"It was your idea to keep separate bank accounts, now I know why." He leans into her face.

"You promised me you wouldn't go to the pokies again after my friend saw you there." He waves his hands in the air spilling more beer on the carpet. "You said, I promise, I will never go to the pokies again. And have counselling."

"The pokies are only a relaxation. I can stop any time."

"I don't believe you." He is silent for a moment. "Paula, I said this before and I am saying it again, you have a problem. Although you deny it, you must get help." The room feels leaden.

When he speaks again his voice is laced with malice. "I wonder what your students and colleagues would think of you if they knew." He walks away. "I should ring Sarah right now and let her know that her mother is a pokies' addict."

She jumps up after him, her voice pleading.

"Please don't involve Sarah."

"Damn you." He upends the remains of the beer on the carpet, leaves the room.

Silent footballers grasp each other and jump up and down in the blue haze.

Paula dabs a tissue over the beer in the carpet.

I must stop gambling. It is harder than I thought it would be to stop.

SIXTY-EIGHT

Breaking through denial
June 2009

PAULA DIALS THE NUMBER, IS PLACED IN A QUEUE.

I feel so ashamed and stupid asking for help.

Paula has strategies. She plans to say she is phoning out of curiosity, for a friend. After the last debacle with Colin, she must show him she is serious about changing.

A female with a gentle voice answers the phone.

"Gamblers Help. How can I help you?"

"I'm inquiring about services for a friend." Paula's voice is confident, crisp, a teacher's voice.

The counsellor lists the services: self-exclusion, referral to face-to-face, on-line counselling. The person on the phone carefully moves the shape of the conversation to a personal one and gently turns the focus on Paula.

"What do you like about gambling?"

Caught unaware, she tells the counsellor that the machines provide excitement. She loves the buzz of winning.

"Are you in debt?"

"It's near $20,000," she admits.

How terrible that sounds when you say it out loud, $20,000...

"Does your partner know?"

Paula is silent for a few minutes.

"Yes, it was my husband who discovered the credit card debt. He said I must get help."

And he will make me suffer forever.

"Do you want face-to-face counselling or connect with a counsellor online?"

Paula thought briefly about using the online service. But knew it would be too easy for her to lie to an invisible counsellor.

"I prefer face-to-face," said Paula.

The woman on the phone is pleasant, encouraging,

"It takes a lot of courage to ring us and get help. The machines trap people and keep them gambling. The bells and whistles are there to grab you," said the counsellor.

"Yes, I have been grabbed," Paula said.

That night she tells Colin she is seeing a counsellor next week.

"I'll come with you."

"I prefer to go alone." Her heart beats fast.

Last thing I need is Colin to make a scene.

~

The following week Paula locates the building, takes the lift to the eighth floor. She looks around the room for a place to hide. Finds a chair near the back. Three women flick through magazines. No one makes eye contact. Paula pretends interest in two pamphlets.

I hope the counsellor is not someone I know.

It crosses Paula's mind to escape, to construct a story that the counsellor become ill and cancelled the appointment, but Colin might check.

"Paula?" a call from an open door.

Here goes.

She is escorted into a pocket-sized office. Two small paintings of Venice adorn the walls. A large window faces an extensive panorama of Melbourne city. St Paul's Cathedral and Flinders Street station clearly visible. The sun shines on the cathedral, making it sparkle.

"My name's Carol," said the counsellor.

"We usually spend the first session getting to know each other and collecting data."

Paula fills in consent, Office of Gambling database, and assessment forms.

I loathe this…I'm in the middle of a nightmare.

"I should have known better than be in this situation," Paula said, her face bright red. "Everyone says that," said Carol, smiling at Paula.

"Many use gambling to separate from reality, then it becomes a habit."

Paula is distracted by Carol's large butterfly patterned dress that skims the floor. She sneaks a peek at Carol's qualifications hanging above the desk.

I hate this. I hate this...

SIXTY-NINE

Getting to the
bottom of things
June 2009

It is four weeks since Paula ventured into any venue that holds pokie machines. She tells herself the gambling was a distraction from Rachael's death.

Colin develops an irritating interest in her weekly gambling counselling sessions, writing down the dates of her appointment and asking endless questions about the session.

"What did you discuss at gambling counselling today?" he said.

The words 'gambling counselling' are elongated in case she misses the significance.

Colin had taken to staring hard in her face, looking for clues of what is under the smile, the calm façade.

I wonder what is going on inside Paula's head?

"We are working on strategies," she said.

"What strategies?"

"Not carrying money with me, staying away from the venues, keeping busy."

The responses sound tame to him.

"Wouldn't everyone who had a gambling problem do the same?"

She acts distracted and vague.

"When can I come with you and give my side of the story to the counsellor?" he said.

"Soon," she said raising her eyebrows.

Never. if I have any say in it.

She is afraid he might blow her cover, unravel the elaborate web of lies she carefully invented to save face from one health professional to another.

Between Colin's watchful eyes and Carol's bright banter, something shifts.

Paula changes her daily routine and walks from an earlier tram stop and takes a shortcut through the park, avoiding the pokie venue.

Does not carry credit cards nor large amounts of cash with her.

She wonders who is playing her favourite polar bears machine.

It's too dangerous to return to the venue just now.

She wouldn't put it past Colin to check and look for her there.

And that stupid friend of his might be there.

"So, what do you think, Paula?" asks Carol. "Are you mindful?"

"Yes, I am aware of being mindful, living in the present."

She watches Carol bend over to pick up a pen. The huge multi-coloured dress blocks the light. She despises the counselling sessions, hates the invasive nature of them.

"How much have you spent on the pokies in the years you have been gambling?"

"Not much," Paula said.

"Would it be $5,000?"

"About that…"

Carol's gaze burns.

"A little more."

They both stare at each other in silence. Paul's face flames.

"You don't like these sessions, do you?" asked Carol.

"My husband made me come."

"Your husband wants to join us in a session. This is helpful for some couples."

Paula closes her mouth and slinks deeper into the chair. "I don't want Colin here."

What she hates is Carol asking about her mother.

"I don't like to discuss her," Paula said, turning pale.

"You are only as sick as your secrets," Carol said. "Let's return to your mother and why you keep changing the topic when I bring it up. Is it too sensitive?"

Paula's hands tremble. Sunlight entering the office reflects her dilated pupils.

"My mother was a formidable woman," she at last.

~

As if the counselling sessions and Colin's interrogation afterwards weren't bad enough, Paula has started seeing shadows of dead people in corners of streets.

Once in the back of a lecture hall, she saw Father. He was crying out to her, "I'm so sorry." Then she blinked, and he was gone.

Another day she caught the reflection of Rachael in the mirror as she washed her hands in the staff toilet. She turned quickly, and a volume of water ran down her blue silk shirt.

Yesterday she glimpsed Doris's face out of the tram window.

"I should have kept you locked in the cupboard," said the shadow.

"Shut up and leave me alone," Paula blurts out.

The young woman sitting next to her on the tram puts down her book and stares.

"That's what I should have said to her," said Paula.

The young woman nods and returns to her reading.

It was all unnerving and made no sense.

SEVENTY

Spring cleaning
July 2009

ONE DAY, PAULA WANDERS THROUGH THE ROOMS OF her house.

Everything in this home needs a good overhaul. I won't touch the garage; it's Colin's turf.

She makes long, detailed lists. Examines every room.

Paula remembers the story of a man who needed a larger home just to house his possessions.

She collects cardboard boxes from the supermarket and green plastic bags.

Armed with a mop and dusters, she starts on the main bedroom cupboards. In a flash, unwanted clothes and shoes pile on the floor. Many of her clothes are now out of fashion.

Colin applauds her efforts and contributes with a pile of stained his T-shirts and socks. The space in the wardrobe enlarges.

She crawls under the bed and pulls out shoe boxes of photos to sort out later.

"Maybe its menopause," Colin said to his brother.

"As long as she doesn't throw you out."

Colin stays out of her way, but every so often Paula finds something to show him.

"Do you remember this ball gown?"

He nods.

She knows he does not.

She holds the blue chiffon against her chest and looks in the mirror. Colin danced every dance with her at that engineering ball all those years ago. She waltzes around the room, then folds the dress into the cardboard box.

Someone will take you to a ball again.

She takes the boxes to the charity shop.

"Spring cleaning?" the volunteer asked.

"Yes, having a good clean out."

The pantry is next.

Paula discards old jelly packets, gelatine, and Gravox gone lumpy. Flips through recipe books stuffed with handwritten notes and cuttings from magazines and throws them in rubbish bin. Keeps the good dinner set and five aluminium saucepans and the heavy frying pans.

Loads cardboard boxes containing fourteen glass jars and twelve mismatched Tupperware containers into her small car. The kitchen shrinks to one-third its size. She scrubs shelves, replaces kitchen paper.

The linen press takes no time to sort. Shabby towels and sheets, odd blankets and doonas folded and packed for the charity shop.

Colin is sure she'll weaken when she comes to sorting the study. She moves out-of-date research and lecture notes straight into the bin. Drags the rubbish skip near the front door and throws full folders of notes without looking at them.

To be efficient in the present, I must remove the clutter from my past.

It takes little effort to clean the computer. Control, Alt, and Delete, and files, emails, and internet sites disappear forever. The hard drive space triples.

She rips up letters, tosses out Christmas cards. The office looks roomy for the first time and develops an echo.

She labels a thin manila folder for important papers and places it on her desk next to the current lecture notes.

The floor-to-ceiling bookshelf in the lounge room is cramped with books, children's games, and photos in pine wood picture frames that require careful sorting.

Unwanted books are taken to the charity shop.

Children's games boxed for a colleague with young children.

The photos removed from their frames and placed in photo albums.

Next Paula hauls the Horn cabinet from against the wall in the study. Both the sewing cabinet and Bernina sewing machine were gifts from Colin. She opens the cabinet and remembers the Knit

Wit course. The Bernina made short work of over-locking tracksuits, T-shirts, and dresses.

Memories flash past of giggling daughters fidgeting as she pinned alterations to the new clothes. They always staged a fashion parade when the garments were done.

Sarah and Rachael modelling her latest creation while Colin clapped.

She remembers awkward doll's clothes and funny hats the girls sewed.

Sarah loved to make elaborate trousers and skirts for her dolls out of the scraps of her own dresses.

I'll keep the sewing machine for Sarah.

She oils it, replaces it back in the cabinet, and pushes it against the wall.

The garden needs work. The small vegetable bed, hidden by a fence of perfumed roses is overgrown with weeds. The parsley has seeded.

There is a towering avocado tree, but no avocados ever fruited. The tree grew enormous from an avocado stone Paula planted when they first came to the house. A forlorn swing hangs off the branches. She weeds, trims until her back aches. She buys a lemon tree and plants it next to the roses.

~

On a warm morning, she drives to Springvale Memorial Garden Cemetery to lay flowers on Rachael's grave. She sits on the milk crate as usual.

My darling Rachael, I miss you more each day.

∽

Thursday night, Paula suggests they eat at Colin's favourite restaurant. Children run around squealing. She makes a point of being agreeable, hanging on his every word. She laughs at his jokes, even those she has heard before.

"This is good pizza," Colin said with his mouth full. "Let's do it again next week."

"Yes," she said. "Let's." She hates pizza.

Colin stops mentioning the counselling sessions. He's pleased with the way things are going.

SEVENTY-ONE

The psychologist
September 2009 Carlton

PAULA'S HEELS *CLICK-CLICK* ON THE PAVEMENT. SHE winds the blue scarf tighter around her neck. Sweet wrappers and McDonald's drink containers dance at her feet. She crunches through the autumn leaves, retrieves a single red plane leaf. It is perfect except for one curled edge.

This is an omen of sorts.

She slips the leaf in her pocket.

She wonders how to present as a person needing help without disclosing too much. How to do this with dignity as one health professional to another?

Paula's sessions with Carol have unleashed flashbacks related to her childhood. The images frighten her. Carol suggested a specialist grief psychologist. And the reason for Paula's appointment with Mary Dorcas today.

"I'm Paula Wilson; my appointment is at nine," she tells the receptionist.

She motions her to sit and hands her a clipboard. "Please complete the admission details."

Paula's hands are cold. It is difficult to write. She is the only person in the waiting room. Two academic degrees in wooden frames hang on the wall. Paula taps her feet, opens and shuts her bag. She glances at her watch. She must teach in two hours.

Where the hell is Mary Dorcas?

Twenty minutes pass. The office door eventually opens and a thirty-ish woman steps out. She is dressed in red from top to toe. Red stretch top, red straight skirt, and red high-heeled shoes stockings. The woman wears large red owl glasses, a slash of bright red lipstick on her lips. A heavy gold chain with a giant diamond encrusted crucifix dangles around her neck. She reeks of Fendi perfume.

"I'm Mary Dorcas." She motions Paula to follow her in to the office.

"What appears to be the problem?"

"I'm a social worker," Paula said, making sure her gaze is direct and voice strong. "I am unsure where to begin." She hesitates, waiting for a response. The office is hot. Paula drapes her coat over her knees.

"My sixteen-year-old daughter died a few years back and I'm having problems coping. I'm frozen in time and place. Afraid to let go. Bottle my feelings up."

Mary Dorcas doesn't speak, never taking her eyes off Paula. After a long silence, she said, "Are you depressed?"

"Yes."

"Do you have suicidal thoughts?"

"Not really…"

Mary Dorcas is silent again.

"I am concerned that you are suicidal. I see the signs in your behaviour.

What signs is she talking about? This woman is an idiot. I walk into the office and tell her my daughter has died. It is normal to be depressed.

Mary Dorcas makes a show of closing the folder with Paula's name on it.

"I recognize the signs," she repeats.

She taps her long red fingernails on the desk.

"You're depressed and admitted to being suicidal. It is my policy when clients mention suicide they must be assessed by a colleague who is a doctor."

She stands up and strides to the door. "After you have seen the doctor you can come back to me and we will work on your grief issues."

"I did not mention suicide; you asked me," said Paula.

"Any suicide ideation needs to be explored and suitable antidepressants prescribed." She purses her red lips. "Please pay for today's session as you go out."

Paula is speechless. She remains seated clutching at her coat, unable to move.

I am no kid off the street to be talked down like that.

Mary holds the door knob until Paula stands to leave.

"Do you want to make another appointment?" asks the woman behind the desk.

"No, thank you."

The waiting room is still empty.

Paula runs to the car. She's engulfed in a foul mood by the time she enters the class.

~

"Today's topic is Post-Traumatic Stress Syndrome. It can take many forms."

Paula clicks through the PowerPoint slides.

"The signs of PTSS can be flashbacks of the traumatic event, feelings of estrangement or detachment, sleep and memory disturbances, avoidance of people, and using addictive behaviours to soothe."

The students scribble notes. A few ask questions.

"My brother Rod was a helicopter pilot in Iraq. He said most of his army friends suffer from Post-Traumatic Stress Syndrome. Every time the news shows video coverage of the war, his PTSS gets worse," said one student.

Paula nods.

"Rod went to an army psychologist once, but he couldn't help him." said the student.

"Any health professional part of the army must reflect the company line," Paula said.

"I understand the defence force is better able to deal with the problem now."

After class, she drives to a pokie venue. It's been a while. She feeds $50 into the first available machine.

Stuff you, Mary Dorcas. I have other ways of coping.

SEVENTY-TWO

The swimming pool
December 2009 Singapore

PAULA FEELS AS THOUGH SHE IS FLYING, THE WATER creating a wind tunnel. She is lost in another dimension. She swims arm over arm, face under and over the water.

Paula is in Singapore for a Social Work conference. Earlier that day she had given details of her latest research project related to Siblings Survivor stress. After the conference, she discovered this community pool near her hotel. The long lanes and clean water tempted her. The small, marble tiled hotel pool with fancy recessed lights was not suitable for serious swimming.

~

She remembers the Australian couple at the airport. They had a son living in Singapore with his family.

"He has a few servants," the woman said in pride. "They have a maid, cook, and cleaner."

"He must live in a large home to need so much help."

"No, they live in an apartment. It is expected of them, the need to show face."

"But not Australians," Paula said.

She considered it bizarre for a tribe of servants keeping house for a family of three.

The older woman said the servants don't work on Sundays. "It's the going rate here. Work from 6 a.m. until 9 p.m."

"That's exploitation in Australia," said Paula.

"This is not Australia."

The older woman is signalled by a customs officer and moves forward.

Paula wonders if people change their standards according to the situation or country they find themselves. She knows her moral compass changed with her gambling and she was able to lie and be deceitful.

≈

Today, something inside of her takes shape; an echo of who she used to be is restored.

There are so many parts of me that have blown away.

The sky is clear, the humidity increases. Unseen birds call to each other. She steps out of the pool, changes into her dress. Hair dripping, wanders into a hawker centre opposite the pool. Orders iced coffee and fried rice.

People stare; she knows she stands out from the local Asian faces.

A wrinkled old man at a nearby table slices cabbage. The table covered in white sliced leaves. Every so often another man clears the vegetable into a cane basket. The old man continues chopping.

Everyone must create meaning in their lives even if it's chopping cabbage.

PART 3

SEVENTY-THREE

Rachael's journal
April 2010

AFTER HER TRIP TO SINGAPORE, PAULA FEELS emotionally strong enough to complete the spring cleaning by tackling Rachael's room. Every room has been thoroughly cleaned and decluttered except this one.

It is mid-morning, the sun streams through the windows in the house. She hesitates. Paula fears the room, wants it to disappear. It is lousy with saturated pain.

Rachael's room has strange powers. Paula seldom enters here since her daughter's death. If she closes her eyes she can almost hear Rachael's voice singing her favourite Rolling Stones songs.

Come on, come on. Let's do it.

She turns the door handle with caution. Tiptoes in. Places the three cardboard boxes, mop, and cleaning agents on the floor. The window is always left slightly open, but still has a stale, thick smell.

Unfathomable feelings lurk here. Time has stood still in the room. Invisible images of Rachael hover. The hair on the back of Paula's neck stands. She shivers.

The room appears harmless with its red cotton spread over the neat bed. The walls cramped with Rolling Stones posters in a time warp. The dressing table piled at one end with three sad-eyed teddy bears and a shaggy elephant.

The pink laptop is closed on the desk.

Books arranged as if they were flung into the shelves from across the room.

Assorted yellowing photos jammed around the dressing table mirror.

Who are these people?

She opens the dressing table drawers and throws socks, jumpers, shirts, and jeans into a box.

That wasn't so bad.

She sighs with relief. Handles the old, hooded blue parka. It was Rachael's favourite. Wore it for years. Paula inhales the parka, it smells of Rachael. Past images slide past. Rachael pulling the parka fur hood over her face until her only eyes were visible. Laughing. She was always laughing then.

The accident changed everything.

She empties the parka pockets, three twenty cent coins, a dollar, sugar sachet, scraps of paper with a scribbled phone number. Paula fingers the paper.

I wonder if it's the drug dealer's phone number?

She folds the jacket and places it in a charity box. Returns to the emptying the contents of the drawer. Her eyes widen, finds an unused syringe still in its package, rolled tightly inside a knitted scarf.

Rachel had an overdose in this room. The paramedics brought her back to life.

Job done...but for us it was the start of a slow death.... Where did she get the drugs?

How did I miss the signs at the beginning when she started using?

She returns to the pile of clothes, pulls the jacket from the charity box, sets it aside. Moves to the open window.

She hears a football being kicked, watches two boys kick the ball to each other. One boy kicks it onto Paula's front yard. She watches him run over her petunias, grab the ball, and kick it back. It bounces onto a parked car.

Why did she start with the drugs? She was never mistreated, only loved and cared by us. No one was locked in a cupboard in this home. I can't accept my beautiful daughter died of a heroin overdose.

Paula lays on the bed and stares at the ceiling.

Rachael was horrible after the overdose. Blamed us for everything. I tried so hard to get her off heroin. How many detox places did I drag her? She didn't want methadone. Refused Suboxone.... I never thought it would be so hard being a parent of a drug using child. Everything was wrong, upside down.... Maybe it was my fault. Maybe I didn't try hard enough.... I wish I had one more day to spend with Rachael. One more chance to change what happened. To fix things. To make things better…. How to live the rest of my life when I am stuck in Rachael's death? How to move forward? I gamble to escape my anger and guilt. Because to think too much is to come face to face with my darkness.

Paula holds her left wrist, rocks back and forth to soothe herself. The room is cool. The curtains move slightly with the incoming breeze. But the thickness in the room stays, is a heaviness like going down a deep well. The air sucked out.

Rachael used to steal from us, go through everyone's pockets and wallets when we weren't watching…. I had to stuff my wallet in my bra…. I hated the trips to Cash Converters. Colin was always angry, always shouting…. You bring up your children with love and do everything for them. You never suspect that one day you will need locks and safes to protect your things from your own child…. What was Sarah doing in the middle of Rachael's drug using chaos? I can't remember, she was so quiet.

Paula closes her eyes. It was still vivid.

The drugs were much worse than the head injury and the madness of PTA…it has been chaotic in this home for years.

"Enough," she said aloud.

"Back to work."

She opens Rachael's music box. A small, pink, dancing ballerina spins around in circles in time to Mozart.

Rachael loved the music box. Played it all the time when she was little.

The innocence and beauty burns deep. Paula snaps it shut.

This is harder than I thought.

She stands on a chair to reach the top cupboard, swishes the damp sponge to the back, feels something, then stops.

What's this?

Something hard. She uses the mop handle to push it to the front. It's a box for boots, wide and hard. She lifts the lid. Gasps, breathes in short bursts. The box reveals more unused syringes, bent spoons, a cigarette lighter, ampules of water, and a tattered exercise book.

She pushes the syringes and drug paraphernalia to one side. Still standing on the chair, opens the notebook. Rachael's writing is large, childlike, in various degrees of illegibility.

"November 10th: I wonder what happened to Doris my tortoise? I used to wash his shell. Dad made a hutch for him.

Dec 3rd: I spilled orange juice on Mother's stupid carpet. 'Rachael take care,' she said in that awful judgemental voice. 'I can't help it, my stupid hand shakes,' I said.

Mother looked at me as if I shit on her shoe. Is the carpet more important to her than me? What about my feelings?"

Paula steps down from the chair. She's afraid to read further but is unable to stop.

"*Dec 7th: I beat Dad at dominoes. 'Rachael, still the best domino player in the world,' he said. We lined them in circles and made them fall again and again. Poor Dad. Mum gives him such a hard time. She picks on him all the time.*"

Paula reddens, brushes the hair from her forehead.

"*Dec 20th: Mum took me shopping for clothes. Nothing fits. 'We must put you on a diet,' she said. Great, my mother considers me fat. Always the criticism, she never stops.*

I loathe her superior tone.

Dec 21st: Sarah and I watched stupid movies all afternoon. We squashed up on the sofa, covered with Gran's old rug. Police Academy movies made us laugh. We made hundreds and thousands of kiddie party sandwiches, had a party. Mother came in from work. Not 'hello girls, how are you?' She went straight into, 'Clean up the mess in the kitchen.'

Mum's a mean bitch. I hate her. Sarah told me she's planning to leave to study in Cambridge. I might go with her.

Dec 22nd: Whose name to write on a Christmas card? Where are my friends?

I have none. My life stinks.

Jan 18th: I made a new friend, someone who doesn't care if I have a disability. 'Hello, H.' Charles gave me a taste a few weeks back, and I was sick. I couldn't understand what the fuss was about. Then the next one as wonderful! I closed my eyes and floated like being in a dream. I loved it.

Feb 20th: Oops. I've been greedy. I have a habit. Shitty. All I care about is the next hit. I stole $50 from Dad's wallet. He didn't notice.

March 3rd: I need to be careful. Took too much H. Ambulance. Narcan shit. I wished I died on that blissful cloud. They know now. It's hell on bloody earth. Mum and Dad watch me all the time. They're on my case day and night. I am not their daughter any more. All they see is heroin. Hey, I'm here, too. A person. I matter.

July 24: Mum dragged me to drug and alcohol detox for an interview. I went along to shut her up. 'Rachael, you have to stop using.' I can't. H doesn't do it for me now. I need it to stop withdrawing.

August 3rd: I took Mum's pearls to Cash Converters, $100 worth of heaven. There was hell to pay when she found out. She never wore those bloody pearls. I needed the money.

August 17th: Dad threw me out again. I stole from his wallet. I banged on the door for a while and met up with Charles. We smoked pot, went to Maccas to wait for Tony.

Mother found me and demanded I go home with her or she'd call the police. She acted like a raving lunatic. I was so embarrassed. I had to leave. She doesn't care about me. She's ashamed her university friends will find out her daughter is a junkie. I hate *her. She pretends she's so high and mighty. She's a hypocrite.*

Paula sat motionless for a long time, staring at the wall.

She quietly replaces the contents in the box and pushes it back in the cupboard.

SEVENTY-FOUR

Email Colin to Sarah
April 2010 Melbourne

HELLO SARAH,

Thanks for the jokes and the photo of Buzz. He's thinner and taller than I imagined. He seems nice enough. Your mother is still throwing things out. Spring cleaning, she said. Demolition derby is what I call it. Last week she went through Rachael's room. I noticed four boxes of clothes and books for the charity shop. It must have been hard for her. She has been rather quiet since. How are you coping with the drizzle and cold weather? Love from your number one man. Dad. Remember Buzz is number two. XX

SEVENTY- FIVE

Email Sarah to Colin
April 2010 Cambridge

DEAR NUMBER ONE MAN, DAD.

It's about time that mum has moved on and thrown out Rachael's stuff. I was afraid she planned to keep the room as a shrine. Did she go through my room? There's not much there. I had a good clear out before I came here. It is warm as toast here in the dorm. But when I go out I need a beanie, scarf, and thick jacket. And wellies. It always rains. Say hello to Mum for me. Tell her she owes me an email. Love you lots, Sarah xx ooo

SEVENTY- SIX

Paula always sleeps with the bedroom door open
May 12, 2010

PAULA CANNOT SLEEP, EYES WIDE OPEN, BODY STIFF. Her heart's thumping, faster, faster, like a galloping horse. Snippets of Rachael's journal running in circles in her head.

I am unravelling like a skein of wool.

The fridge downstairs turns itself off to defrost with a shuddering *clomp*. Birds stir in the gum tree outside. The house creaks as it cools. Possums clamber over the roof.

Is the net over the apple tree? Damn possums take one bite from the apples and drop them to the ground below...

A car stops, male voices drift in the moonlight, doors bang. The neighbour's spoiled cat yowls, scratches. The neighbour's door opens, scolds the cat, and closes the door with a bang.

The stupid cat digs in my garden.

Paula sleeps with the bedroom door open, hating the intensity of a shut door. She makes sure a window is open as well, even though Colin complains.

She throws back the doona, is sweating, burning. A few minutes later she is cold and shivering pulling the covers. Turns to watch Colin, marvelling he can sleep so no matter what's happening. Wants to jab him in the ribs, make him suffer with her. But does not. What good would it do?

I wish I had his knack for sleeping. He was like that after Rachael died. I tossed and turned but he slept.

"It's no good both of us tearing our hearts apart. Anyway, I need my sleep," he had said.

Paula fights the urge to push Colin out of bed, shove him and watch him wake. How many times has she tried to talk to him? He never paid attention, walked away.

"You work it out; you're the one with the social work degrees," he had said.

It's difficult to figure anything out these days. Her mind clogged.

Colin makes alarming little grunts and snorts.

I wonder what he's dreaming?

The curtains flap in and out in time with the breeze, a rhythmic orchestra. Her eyes stare at the ceiling. Twenty minutes later she slides from the double bed, pulls on the dressing gown, creeps down the stairs.

She checks the tattered envelope she has been carrying around for the last fortnight. Most items have a line through them.

Better make a move.

The kitchen fills with coffee aroma, pours the steaming liquid, encloses the cup with her hands. The soft dawn changing the hollow darkness.

She sniffs the sweetness of the morning.

My life never went to plan. Something always got in the way.

Paula picks her mobile phone, sends a text message to Sarah in Cambridge.

"Happy Friday. What are your plans for the weekend?"

A text returns. "Swotting, a big exam next week. No plans but to study."

Paula responds with, "Good luck. Love you, my beautiful Sarah."

A smiley face as reply. "Love you, too."

The kitchen is peaceful, Paula's favourite room.

How many meals have I cooked here? I remember when the girls were young how they loved to cook with me. White flour covering every surface. Little feet and floury footsteps on the floor. Pink icing for cupcakes licked from spoons.

She smiles, inhaling the memory.

At 6 a.m. she collects the newspaper. It has been drizzling overnight, the plastic wrapper sprays water as she unravels it. Takes the paper to Colin with a fresh cup of coffee.

"Ohhh," he says as the light shines on his face. He covers his head with the pillow.

"Time to wake." She said.

"I had a strange dream. You disappeared into thick fog and I couldn't find you," he said.

"Lucky you."

"No, it was a nightmare."

She kisses him. "I'm here."

Paula retreats to the study. Shuts the door holding her breath. She alters the answering machine message for her phone at the university.

She checks the message, "You have rung Paula Wilson's extension. I am unavailable to take your call. Please ring Gina Rhodes on extension 2876 for any inquires related to second year social work student issues."

She waits for the shaking to stop. Breaths deeply. Retrieves the scrappy envelope from the pocket, ticks off two items.

Keep going. No turning back now.

She holds the desk to steady herself.

Paula moves through the house upstairs and down, taking in the space, order and cleanliness.

I love everything ordered.

She returns to the kitchen, checks the freezer, fifteen blue topped containers stacked, dated and labelled. Last Saturday, she cooked the whole afternoon. Reads the labels as she touches the lids.

Beef Lasagne, chicken casserole, lamb casserole, sweet and sour, meatballs and sauce, meatloaf, apple pie, lentil and vegetable soup. There should be enough for a fortnight of main meals. He can organize a sandwich for lunch.

The laundry baskets are empty. She stood ironing for three hours on Sunday. The old musical *Singing in the Rain* with Gene Kelly was on TV.

～

She remembers Aunt Bertha taking her to the musical as a birthday treat when she was a child. They ate chocolate ice cream at interval and bought black liquorice squares that coated your tongue. They linked arms on the way home and sang.

"I'm singing in the rain, getting soaking wet," They swung around lamp posts.

Dear Aunt Bertha, I was happy around you. When you died, you took the best part of my childhood.

She frowns, remembers her mother made a furious fuss about Paula's scuffed white shoes when they returned home.

"You ruined your shoes!" Doris had shouted.

～

Paula showers, peers into the foggy mirror. Wipes a space on fog on the glass. There are deep wrinkles around her eyes. Pulls the skin back to smooth them. Applies foundation, eyeliner, lipstick, and powder. Sprays with perfume. She dresses in her best black suit. The one with the fitted jacket and sleek black slacks. She adds a white shirt. She collects the black briefcase and handbag.

"I'm off," she said going to Colin.

Colin is in bed, reading the paper. "You look nice," He likes seeing her in a suit.

She gives him a long hug and kisses him.

"Are you all right?" he asks. "Have you been crying?"

"I have been thinking about Rachael..." she said.

He says nothing, nods.

"I will be late tonight. The Seminar might go on a while. I made lasagne and a salad. Microwave it for three minutes."

"Okay."

"Love you," she said. Goes back and hugs him again.

Her high heels clatter down the stairs, past the borders of red and pink petunias, past the old gum tree to the street.

Crowds spill onto footpaths. She crosses the pedestrian crossing at Racecourse Road and walks to Pin Oak Crescent. She passes the hairdressers, McKillop family centre, dental surgery and medical centre in Pin Oak crescent. Then up the steep ramp to Newmarket station. Her breathing is laboured, hands sweating.

So many people.

The Metro train is in the distance.

Walks to the end of the platform.

She waits until the train is closer.

She jumps in its path.

The burst of pain. A sharp compression jammed against her legs and chest. She opens her mouth to cry out but folds into darkness as the unyielding whack of cold metal and steel, crushing, pushing her forward, then nothingness, blackness.

SEVENTY-SEVEN

Sam Redina
May 12, 2010

IT IS EARLIER IN THE SAME DAY OF MAY 12ᵀᴴ AT 5 A.M. in Brunswick.

Sam Redina is wearing the dark blue silk dressing gown Eva bought him for Christmas. The dressing gown hangs untied, showing his stripy underpants. At forty-six, he's still a handsome man. He is contemplating leaving Eva, his wife of twenty years. He's met someone else, who makes him young again. Thinking about Ann makes him sentimental. She has warm, soft skin, honey blonde hair, baby voice. He's Superman with Ann. She cannot keep her hands out of his pants.

"What's the matter?" Eva stirs, aware Sam is moving.

"Just the burning in my gut...go back to sleep," he said in Italian.

He enters their small, neat kitchen. Fills the espresso machine, puts it to gas stove, and waits for it to bubble. Lights a cigarette. Opens the door, checks on his capsicums. They're green and healthy.

His tomatoes are not doing so well, attacked by a red bug.

White oil for the tomatoes.

Sam collects *The Herald Sun*. He drinks his coffee black, eats a sweet bun, showers, and dresses in his Metro uniform.

He's been a train driver for ten years; he is a careful and astute driver. His father came from Calabria and worked in a paint factory until his death.

"Goodbye," he said.

"I'll be home late, no need to wait."

"Mmmm" she said.

When he completes his shift today, Sam and Ann are meeting in her flat in Coburg. He has a surprise for her tucked away near the spare wheel in his car. It's a gold chain with a gold frog. A foolish gift but she will love it.

He listens to the radio 3AW on the way to work. Parks the white Commodore at the Metro rail yards. Ted is the controller on duty. Sam is on the standby shift today. Checks the daily roster.

"Not the Craigieburn line again," Sam said, his voice rising in annoyance. "Why am I doing the Craigieburn line today?"

"John's sick," said Ted.

"John's always sick."

Sam locates the train, a silver Comeng with six carriages. He climbs into the engine cabin, completes the morning departure check. Another driver has already prepared the train. Sam will drive out of North Melbourne rail yards, then through the city loop, stopping all stations to Craigieburn.

He wonders what Ann is doing.

He sends a text. "Remember our date tonight," he wrote.

She responds, "Big sloppy kisses."

He grins.

At Craigieburn station, Sam sets the brake system and prepares to drive back to the city.

At 7.15 a.m., he drives into Newmarket station. The platform is crammed with men and women in suits. He catches sight of her. The woman leans out from the platform. As he gets closer, to his horror, she jumps in front of the train.

He slams the brakes but knows he's hit her. Sam presses the emergency button on the train radio, notifies the controller.

Back at the Metro, Ted starts the emergency procedures and alerts ambulance, police, SES services, bus line, and rings the allocated Metro counsellor.

No trains will go up or down the Craigieburn line until much later in the day.

Sam steps out of the driver's cabin, onto the tracks.

God help me.

He crosses himself. Knows too well that people jump, but the first time it has happened to him.

A severed bleeding leg lies near the train wheel.

A black briefcase half jutting between the wheels. A woman is jammed under the front, contents of her bag and briefcase shredded along the track.

He turns his head and vomits.

Oh, my God.

He's been trained in vigorous emergency procedures. Tries to find a part of the woman to take a pulse. She's alive. His fingers smear with blood. He wipes them on his trousers.

"An ambulance is coming, hang on," he said. Sam shakes; sweat runs down his face. His gut turning and burning.

Two police arrive, one steps down with Sam. The other officer tells the people on the platform, "Please step back."

A siren signals the ambulance's arrival. Two paramedics run up the Newmarket ramp and jump on to the tracks. They carry heavy bags. They assess the situation, ring for support, and notify the Royal Melbourne Hospital emergency department. It's a category one situation.

The paramedics insert an intravenous drip into the injured woman. One paramedic holding the plastic flask, tubing snaking its way to the woman. The other paramedic shines a torch under the train. Loud sirens herald emergency vehicles.

Other passengers oblivious to the drama, walk up the steep slope to reach the station. The policeman puts his hand up.

"There's been an incident, trains will not be

leaving from Newmarket station. Buses will leave from there." He points to the bus stop.

He walks the length of the train with a loud hailer.

"Please get out of the train, it is not running, sorry for any inconvenience. Buses will run. Metro apologies for any inconvenience."

The mood of the crowd turns ugly. In their ignorance, they will complain to Metro. Missives sent to the newspapers complaining about the service.

Eight passengers on the opposite platform stand transfixed in horror. Hands over mouths. They have witnessed the incident. Shake their heads in disbelief. The older officer climbs to the platform. They mill around him. He takes notes, collects witness details.

"A bus will take passengers. Could you move off the platform now? Thank you."

Newmarket station is chaos and flashing lights. Heavy machinery is manoeuvred onto the tracks to lift the train off the injured woman.

Grim-faced motorcycle police escort the ambulance to the hospital.

Sam is interviewed, drug tested, and breathalysed. His story is reviewed with those of eyewitness.

Detailed reports must be produced. Many pages written, photos taken, accurate maps drawn. The coroners' court is demands accuracy in every detail.

As per the manual, Sam climbs into taxi to the Metro trauma counsellor.

He rings Eva.

SEVENTY-EIGHT

Natalie Baxter
May 12, 2010

It is earlier in the day of the same day May 12th at 5:30 a.m. in Carlton.

Natalie Baxter rolls over. Checks the clock radio time. Is soon under the shower singing.

"I'm getting married in the morning, ding dong the bells are going to chime...."

She dries herself noticing a flabby abdomen.

I need to lose weight.

Pulls her thick black hair into a scrunchie. At thirty-eight, she's not beautiful in the classical sense, but moves like a ballerina in quick little bursts.

Earlier, Natalie spoke to Neil, her fiancé, by Skype. He's stationed in Iraq. Neil is a doctor in a forty-bed burn and trauma unit, for Medecins Sans Frontieres in the city of Suleimaniyah.

"Nats, will you marry me in Fitzroy Gardens when I come home for leave? A small wedding just you and me, and your mum and dad and my mum."

"Yes."

"And let's have a baby straight away," he said.

"Not so sure about that," she laughed.

Natalie switches the kettle on. She places a green tea bag into a cup. Puts two pieces of brown, wholemeal bread into the toaster. Fresh eggs are dropped into the saucepan covered with water. She eats the breakfast looking out at her small Carlton courtyard.

I'll wear a strapless pink dress for the wedding.

Lilac scent floats in the morning freshness. She glances at her watch.

No time for dilly-dallying.

She throws the dishes in the sink, covers them with a blue tea towel and rushes out the door.

Natalie is the Nurse Unit Manager in the emergency department. She lives fifteen minutes from the hospital.

Receives the nursing handover from Margaret the night-duty nurse manager.

"It's quiet now. But was full on most of the night," said Margaret.

Few patients are left in the cubicles. The others transferred to short stay ward or hospital wards. Most discharged home.

"Cubicle four, Mrs Johnston, eighty-nine, fell out of bed last night. X-rays revealed fractured right neck of femur. She's awaiting transfer to theatre, fasting."

Her daughter dozes next to Mrs Johnston.

"I need to milk the cows...." said Mrs Johnston.

"We gave her 30 mL of Morphine at 5 a.m.," Margaret said as a means of explanation.

Cubicle eight appears empty at first glance. A small human is half-covered under a white sheet. Crepe bandages wound around her arms.

Margaret drops her voice.

"This is Marty, seventeen. Last night had a fight with her boyfriend Gill. Cut herself six times with a razor in the forearms; not too bad but needs suturing. Dr Raymond is preparing the suture trolley. We called Marty's mother, but she isn't responding. No sign of Gill either. The psyche registrar is coming in at 9:30 for the mental health assessment."

Marty slides further under the sheets.

"In this cubicle we have Joseph, fifty-nine. Last evening while watering his garden, he had an allergic reaction to an unknown insect. The right foot swelled to twice its size. We started him off on antihistamines and he comes off observations at eight. Joseph is on his back snoring.

"His wife will collect him up after she gets the grandchildren off to school."

Natalie and Margaret check the Dangerous Drugs in the DD cupboard, all tallied.

"I am off then..." said Margaret.

Natalie hums as she moves around the department checking emergency equipment. She allocates the nurses to specific cubicles and tasks. Speaks to Harriet the ward clerk. Locates the two male orderlies. Organises the treatment nurse to aid the doctor with the sutures.

The red ambulance phone rings at her desk. Natalie stops humming.

"OK...OK...." She scribbles details on a pad and musters the nursing staff.

"We have a Category One coming. A middle-aged woman has been struck by a train. She's in a critical condition. She has one leg severed, possible abdominal and head injuries. The paramedics placed her in an induced coma at the site. She should be here in ten minutes."

The available staff prepare the main treatment room. Natalie informs key senior staff, organ donor nurse, and priest. The phone rings again, the nursing supervisor is sending extra nurses.

Twelve minutes later, two police officers in black motorbike jackets stride into the emergency department. The ambulance entrance opens, paramedics rush in pushing a trolley with the motionless woman, intravenous attached. They hand over a plastic bag with the right bloodied leg, still with the black boot. Under the trolley are the remains of the woman's mangled handbag and briefcase.

The patient is whisked to the Resuscitation cubicle. Doctors yell orders, nurses run back and forth, one nurse writes the details of all medication as given. The cacophony of noise and activity increases. Running and machinery being wheeled.

Natalie leans over the woman. Swollen eyes taped closed. Blood oozes from bandages. " C a n you hear me? Please squeeze my hand," Natalie asks.

There is no response. She didn't expect one.

The police have already been to the woman's home. No one was home.

Natalie rings the home phone number. A male voice answers.

"Is that Mr Colin Wilson?"

"Yes."

"Are you the husband of Mrs Paula Wilson?"

"Yes, I am," he said.

"My name's Natalie Baxter. I'm the Nurse Unit Manager of the Royal Melbourne Hospital Emergency department."

Silence.

"Are you there, Mr Wilson?" She is gentle.

"Yes. What's wrong?" Mr Wilson's voice loses volume.

"Mr Wilson, I'm very sorry to inform you but a train hit your wife this morning at Newmarket station. She's critically ill. Can you come to emergency department now?"

"I was out for my morning walk..." he said and stops.

Her voice is soft, "Can someone drive you to the hospital or can you take a taxi?"

She knows that road accidents often occur as people rush in, blind with shock.

"Is my wife alive?"

"Yes, come to the Triage nurse's desk and ask for Natalie Baxter."

She puts the phone down.

Colin Wilson tugs at his navy tracksuit. Rings for a taxi. Locks the house. Waits on the curb for the taxi.

He reaches for his mobile phone. He presses Sarah's number in London.

She answers.

SEVENTY-NINE

Night sounds
May 2010

PAULA IMAGINES SHE'S ROWING A CANOE USING JUST her hands. The harder she thrashes in the water, the more the canoe slips back.

Something metallic drops and bounces. It pierces her eardrums, a bell pealing.

God, no. I'm alive.

"Are you in pain?" asks a voice.

And the darkness falls on her again.

EIGHTY

Home sweet home
August 2010

IT'S BEEN FIVE MONTHS SINCE THE TRAIN INCIDENT. Paula is home. The house in Westbourne Street struggles with normality, is again in turmoil. Small birds hop here and there on the lawn. The trees are leafless. Petunias long dead. Local community papers lie rolled in plastic. Bits of paper and leaves litter the ground.

An empty rubbish bin lies on its side, its green lid a gaping mouth. The heavy, grey silk curtains that face the street are pulled across to block out the world.

Inside is dark and gloomy. Antiseptic hits the nostrils. Newspapers and half-drunk coffee cups litter the dining table. A wooden clipboard with a tied pen is covered with scribbled notes.

A shaft of light creeps in from the kitchen window that faces the backyard.

The elegant lounge has morphed into a makeshift sick room. Next to the closed curtains stands a sturdy hospital bed with a solid iron hand rail above. The side table is awash with bottles of medicines, lotions, and tissues. And a photo of two smiling girls in a white frame.

A commode chair is pushed by the wall. A wheelchair parked next to it. The lounge chairs piled to one side to make space. A wooden board lies on the floor. The board is placed to the wheelchair to elevate Paula's stump when she sits. Grab bars are inserted in the downstairs toilet and small bathroom. The woven rugs rolled out of sight.

A temporary bed lies to the side. This is Colin's bed at night. Paula calls out at several times during the night. He needs to be near.

"Colin...," a pleading voice comes out of the darkness.

His body jerks awake. These days he always wears the old navy tracksuit. Colin pulls himself off the low, fold-up bed and switches on the lamp.

"Please help me to roll over," Paula said.

I feel so guilty waking him up. How I hate this. Poor Colin.

He knows what to do. Has done this many times. Colin places the three pillows to one side of Paula's bed, tugs at the lamb wool rug, and rolls her. Paula lets out a cry and clings to the hand rail to steady herself. He makes her comfortable, replaces the pillows behind her and under her stump. He hands her a glass of water. She takes two sips and swallows two tablets.

"Thank you" she said. She runs a shaky hand over his face. "I don't deserve you."

He has a five-day unshaven bristle. Paula notices the dark circles under his eyes. She pretends to close her eyes as if asleep but cannot.

Colin returns to his bed. Switches the light. He stares at the darkness.

Will it ever get better? He thinks.

I wish I was dead. I hate my life, she thinks.

The hammer blow of guilt follows. She drowns in remorse. Each day is the same.

She recalls snippets of her life. Abusive childhood. Rachael. Sarah. Colin. Even Rodney.

Rodney was a self-obsessed narcissist. I must have been mad.

A pokie venue image comes to mind.

Why did I obsess with the pokies? All the wasted time and money lost. For what? I don't know...I've been a fool.

Her chest feels tight.

Maybe it's the morphine. The last thing I want is to become addicted. It blocks the pain. A shield between realities. Was heroin Rachael's shield?

She glances over at Colin, knows he's awake.

"I appreciate everything you do for me," she said. "I'm so sorry to put you through this. The last thing I wanted was to be a burden."

The air is thick with unspoken words.

"I couldn't bear to lose Rachael and you," he said.

She reaches to the side table and touches the tatty yellow ribbon with the red spots that was on Rachael's plaits the time of the accident. It has been with her every day since that terrible day. A keepsake of normal. When life was predictable and safe.

She rolls and unrolls the ribbon. Her eyes moisten. Places it back.

Drifts in and out of sleep.

Wakes with a jolt. Again, she dreamt of Rachael's body in the morgue.

～

When Paula was in the hospital, the train drivers Sam and his wife Eva requested permission to visit Paula in hospital. He told her that his therapist thought it would help him gain closure.

Trendy psychobabble. There's no closure to anything. Things are never resolved, Paula thinks.

Sam and Eva gripped hands, afraid to let go. They stood erect as though bracing themselves for an assault. Fear written over their faces. Eva carried a basket of bright marigolds.

"These are for you."

"Thank you."

The hospital room resembled a florist's shop.

The flowers should've been for my funeral.

"I did everything in my power to stop the train," Sam said.

I wish you hadn't.

"It's not your fault." Paula's voice unemotional.

"I'm glad you're alive," Eva blurted.

I wish I was dead.

"To lose a child can make a person crazy," said Sam. He had tears in his eyes. Eva squeezed his hand.

I wonder who told them about Rachael?

No one spoke.

"Is this the first time your train ever hit anyone?" Paula said.

"Yes, and the last. I'm not driving trains anymore."

I've ruined a man's life. Paula closes her eyes.

∾

Paula is mortified Sarah knows about her incident. She can imagine Sarah telling Buzz.

"My mother tried to kill herself."

She winces at the effect on her daughter. Guilt oozes into everything.

∾

Sarah can't comprehend why her mother would want to commit suicide. She can't imagine her strong, assertive mother at such a low emotion.

To throw yourself in front of a train is gross. How will she cope with one leg? How will she get up the stairs?

Sarah wishes she could be home to help her father but is forbidden to fly. She's pregnant and ill with high blood pressure. The vomiting has been going on for months. She spends much of the day in bed.

Buzz is excited to be a father and suggests a register office wedding.

Sarah is fearful of marriage under the circumstances. She will miss the final exams as the baby's birth is expected in the middle. Won't graduate with Buzz and their friends. She plans to resume her studies after the baby is born. They are still a couple, but their life is not so carefree. The holiday plans to South America are shelved. She doesn't view Cambridge as a wonderful place anymore. They move from the university dormitory and rent a small damp and cold flat. Green fungus flourishes in the bathroom. The wind whistles through the gaps in the window frames.

Sarah has reverted to her old name. Roo doesn't seem right.

She rings home most days. Not only to inquire about her mother but for herself. Pregnancy is frightening.

~

"How are you today?" Sarah asks, her voice artificially light.

How do you talk to your mother when she has tried to kill herself? Should I mention the stump?

"I'm fine, I guess," said Paula. She makes polite

conversation, asks questions. She's surprised that Sarah is pregnant. It makes no sense. Her own two pregnancies were well-planned.

Sarah and Rachael were beautiful babies. I hope Sarah makes a better go of motherhood than I did. We come from a long line of bad mothers. I wasn't like Doris but made my own mistakes. I wonder if Sarah views me as a monster as I did with my mother.

"I'll hand you to Colin." She offers him the phone.

He moves to the kitchen, out of earshot.

"Your mother's struggling. I'm afraid to leave her alone."

"Oh, Dad. I wish I could help."

∾

Max and Barbara know about the suicide attempt. They make frequent, brief visits and leave hot casseroles and cake.

The lack of sleep and stress clouds Colin's judgement. He speaks to Max several times a day. It's the only way he can stay sane.

"You need a break. You're not Superman. Barbara can come and stay with Paula and you and I can have a beer," said Max.

∾

Jenny, Adriana, and Daniel ring. Colin gives a short update.

"No don't visit yet. She's not up to visitors. No, she can't come to the phone. I'll tell you when. Yes, will pass on your messages."

◡

Paula will never return to the University. Word has gone out. She's discussed and stripped bare, exposed.

"Did you hear about Paula?" The story is relayed and embellished along the line. She's the hot topic of conversation in the staff room at lunch time. There's gleeful retelling of the accident. The gossip vultures click their tongues.

"How terrible," they said. The practice of dissecting another's misfortune protects against the reality of their own problems. Paula's entire family history is rehashed. Others, more compassionate, are sad.

"Poor Paula."

Some add, "I never liked her."

◡

Paula loathes being a patient. Every day nursing staff from the 'Hospital in the Home Program' make professional visits. They replace the Baxter Pump with new intravenous fluids. Change dressings. Take temperature, blood pressure. Check the Peripherally Inserted Central Catheter (PICC tube). Adjust analgesia levels. Collect samples of blood.

She watches as an outsider not in her body.

A psychiatrist is allocated when she improves.

No one mentions the suicide attempt. The topic is a dark sea, full of biting sharks. Everyone wonders when she will try to kill herself again.

While the nurses do their work, Colin sits on the back porch. He's troubled by his thoughts. It worries him that everything about Paula was a lie, orchestrated.

Who is the real Paula?

The prickling sensation in his throat is always there. He had no idea she was fragile. Blames himself. Should have known she wasn't traveling well after Rachael's death. Been more observant when she discarded precious things. His fists clench. His eyes blur. He bites his nails. They are bitten to the quick.

This is a chance to fix things, make them right. I wish I knew know what to do.

Carol the gambling counsellor has spoken to Colin. He's learning about grief and the gambling trajectory. It still galls him; so much money is gone.

Daniel enlarges on the historical abuse Paula suffered as a child. It horrifies Colin that Doris could have been so cruel.

Why did Paula try so hard with the old battle axe?

He has never seen Paula cry. Now she cries all the time.

How to get my wife back? Will she try to kill herself again?

The neat, even superficial, pieces of their joined lives are eroded away.

Colin has not been near his garage for weeks. The orders pile.

Tomorrow.

But when tomorrow comes, he sits in the garage and cries, unable to work.

He does what he can for Paula. He checks the dressings and stump. Assists with toileting, heats up Barbara's stews and casseroles. He cleans. Helps with toileting and showing. Checks the IV tubing is not twisted. Deals with the pain medicine.

Her pain rips his gut.

He has no anger towards her.

~

Yesterday; after the nurses fixed the dressings on Paula's stump and changed the Baxter intravenous pump tubing, Colin folded the wheelchair and placed it in the back of the Ute. He carried Paula to the car. She was light to lift.

"A gust of wind and you'll blow away," he said.

He adjusted the seat belt to fit the tiny frame. Brought a thermos of hot coffee and Tim Tam biscuits. Careful to avoid any bumps on the road. Held his hand over her body to prevent her slipping forward when they turned on the roundabout.

They stopped at Williamstown beach. He

pushed the wheelchair to the pier. Paula's single leg hidden by Aunt Bertha's crocheted throw-blanket.

The squawking seagulls hung around ever hopeful for a morsel.

Colin held Paula's hand; they watched the waves in silence.

EIGHTY-ONE

One day at a time
September 2010

LIFE ROTATES IN A CIRCLE. PROBLEMS COME TOGETHER and fall apart. They don't get resolved but reappear again and again in another form. Paula was once the carer, overwhelmed with Rachael's issues. Now she receives care and understands, at a deep level, what Rachael experienced.

The outpatient rehabilitation van now collects Paula three times a week. Her wheelchair hoisted on board and she disappears for the day.

Colin sips his coffee, reads the paper at length and breathes.

Paula is fitted for a prosthetic leg, learns to transfer, and can go to the toilet by herself. She follows the instructions by the occupational therapist and physiotherapist. Struggles with faulting steps. It is difficult to move with the new leg, clings to the walking-bar. Shuffles the length of the bar, collapses in the chair at the end. Hauls herself up with gritted teeth, tries again. One memorable morning she walks the full distance without holding onto the bar.

"Well done," said the physiotherapist.

Paula beams. Dust particles caught in the sun dance near the window. Every painful step is bringing her closer to her grandchild.

She's part of the broken now. There's no gap between her journey and others with disability and illness. At morning tea, Paula positions her wheelchair next to the diabetic Indian lady who is an amputee. There's little English language between them. They sip tea and nibble on Marie biscuits like old friends, gaining power from each other. Their shared vision, to slip back into the functioning life, that has no place for frailty.

～

Barbara drops in at Paula's house on the rehab-free days. She does not waste time with false sympathy.

"You must come to bingo with me." Barbara said.

"It will be part of your training to sharpen your listening skills."

They laugh.

"I'm serious," said Barbara. "You need a hobby. Why don't you volunteer somewhere?"

"I don't think so," said Paula.

～

Colin sleeps in his own bed upstairs now. Paula's goal is to negotiate the stairs, so they can sleep together.

Tuesday morning, Colin tells her, "You have a visitor."

"Hello, sweetheart," said Jenny. She holds a cake box.

"Adriana and I plan to hire a taxi van and take you to Highpoint next week. Let me know what day suits. You need a new dress and jazzy boots to go with your new leg."

Paula frowns. She is not ready. Not yet.

Jenny ignores the lack of interest.

"Bill and I are a couple now. Sounds serious, doesn't it? He hasn't popped the question." said Jenny.

"He's the man I want. Handsome, sexy, and rich."

"A kind man that gets up to the babies at night when you're too tired is a better choice. Even if you are an utter fool and is still there for you," Paula said.

"Like Colin?"

"Yes."

"Sarah emailed me. She's getting married in a registry office."

"She's pregnant," said Paula.

"And you'll be a grandmother."

Colin carries a tray of tea and Monto Carlo biscuits.

"As soon as we can manage the flight, we'll go to England. Visit Sarah and Buzz and meet our grandchild."

Paula notes the graceful lines of Colin's smiling face.

I wonder what Colin is thinking? It must be hard to for him. I never expected him to be there for me. Perhaps he was there all the time and I never noticed. Too wrapped up in my own life to see what was under my own nose.

EIGHTY-TWO

Becoming authentic
October 2010

THE PSYCHIATRIST'S BUSHY GREY EYEBROWS ARCH. He peers unblinking.

"You don't speak the truth Paula," he said.

"I am honest."

"I don't think so. Your words and actions are out of sync. You say what you think I want to hear."

Paula stiffens, opens her mouth to speak but closes it.

"To be authentic, you need to be open to the truth at every opportunity. No matter how unpleasant. Or the ramifications. Every lie you say diminishes you."

He watches her face.

"Your suicide attempt came at the tail end of a long streak of lies about your gambling. I suggest you get a small notebook and jot down every time you catch yourself being untruthful. I want you to bring the notebook next time we meet."

He scribbles a note on the file. He looks at her.

"Is this too simple? Perhaps you were expecting

a magnificent rendition of Attachment Theory and motherhood?" His lips hold a glimmer of a smile.

"What are your thoughts on the homework?"

"It sounds all right," she said.

"Already you aren't honest. Your face indicates annoyance. Your body says frustration. Yet your words said something else."

Paula grimaces.

～

The homework proved difficult. Simple questions like, "How are you today?" from Colin became a minefield.

"I wish I'd died. I'm sorry to put you through this," she said.

The smile drains from his face. She knows the words sting.

"I'm practicing telling the truth. Doctor's orders." She pauses. "I love you, and that is the truest thing I have ever said in my life."

He kisses her on the forehead. "Everything will get better. It takes time. When you hold our little grandchild, you'll be happy."

～

The Boathouse restaurant's wide windows overlook the river. Barbara and Paula sip their wine.

"Trevor misses Rachael. We all loved it when she came around. I miss her," Barbara said.

"You aren't the only one grieving." She coughs.

"Rachael had such a delightful, smart mouth. I wanted to adopt her as my own. Max used to say, 'Let's kidnap her.' Even when she was acting weird with the drugs she was still our girl."

"You knew about the heroin that long ago?" asked Paula.

"How could you not know?" Barbara's eyes narrow.

"Rachael badgered me for money. I said no way was I paying for drugs. Trevor wised up." Barbara looks at the river.

"Colin told me how much effort you put in to getting her help. He couldn't do a thing."

"I see her face everywhere," said Paula.

They sit in comfortable silence.

"I used to think you looked down your nose at our family. You never took time to know us," Barbara said.

"I was a fool. A stupid idiot," said Paula.

"Why were you so judgmental about my bingo when you were playing the pokies? Isn't all gambling the same?" She looks closely at Paula.

"I doubt if I've ever been genuine about anything in my life," said Paula.

She taps the spoon against the salt shaker.

"I find it difficult to be honest. Maybe that's why I kept so many secrets. When I was a child, I told fibs to stay out of trouble. Then later, as an adult, lied to present myself better." She stops. "It matters what people thought of me," gives a half laugh that sounds like a snort.

"Now my life is an open book," bumps the spoon. It falls to the floor.

Barbara bends to retrieve the spoon.

"I'm no expert. I tell Trevor to be straight with me and I won't scream and carry on. I try to be real to him and Max. If I am pissed off with them, I will say it out loud. But at least they don't have to second guess what I am thinking." She leans to Paula.

"Own up to being human."

"I don't know where to start. It's easy for you. You can speak your mind and people still like you…. Rachael thought I was a monster." Her eyes wrinkle in pain.

"No, she didn't." said Barbara.

"I found her diary when I was cleaning her room, no doubt about it, she hated me. That's what set me off to try to kill myself. I couldn't bear it that the person I tried so hard to help and loved so much…hated me to such an extent. Something died inside of me. It crystallised that I was a waste of space and should die."

Paula looked down at her hands. Silent tears run done her face. She wipes them with the palm of her hand.

They are both silent.

"It's just a teenager's vent. I used to say ghastly

things about my mother. But I still loved her." Barbara touches Paula's shoulder.

"In all the years she came to our house, Rachael never uttered a bad word about you."

"My mother loathed me. I hate myself," said Paula. Her eyes glisten, her brow creases.

"Your mother was cruel. Even Colin said she was a piece of work."

"Doris made everyone's life miserable. My father, brother, me. What terrifies me is that I have been as monstrous to my family," said Paula.

"Stop the pity talk. Sarah loves you. Colin adores you. He told Max you were the best thing that happened to him," said Barbara. "Maybe you need to learn to accept yourself as you are." She peers at her watch. "Let's pay the bill. I'll drop you home. I better hurry as Trevor's train will be in soon." She helps Paula get up.

"Next time we meet, we'll practice saying horrible things to each other. It will be lesson 101 in truth," she said.

~

The imaginary fence between mother and daughter has disappeared. Paula doesn't view herself as Sarah's mother. A grandmother, yes. She has given up the mother role by her actions.

They Skype every few days. Sarah gives birth to

a boy. Paula delights in baby Simon. He's a placid little fellow, sleeps and eats on cue.

Sarah dresses him in the clothes Paula sends, even the pink cardigan she knitted.

Buzz completed his degree. He has a tutoring position in the Anthropology department and is contemplating a master's degree. There's no mention about Sarah completing her studies. It doesn't seem so important now.

And Paula does not ask.

~

Today, in the kitchen, Paula pulls herself onto the high stool. All the ingredients are measured and placed in neat order in front of her. She rolls the pastry for the Cornish pasties, Colin's favourite.

So many things to learn with the prosthesis. I must balance my body better. I am so unsteady.

She finds the new leg confronting. Her other injuries have healed. The stump stands in judgment. She can't escape from what she has done. It is all new and complex, must make elaborate plans for every activity.

It seems a lifetime ago she clawed herself up to be someone, a person of respect. An academic, a worthy person. Although she cared for disabled people in her work, she never dreamed she would be one. She is profoundly sad. Not only for what she has lost but what she has become. Guilt and shame linked. She wants to withdraw from the world.

She thinks of the occupational therapist's words.

"Every amputee is different, and you need to work at being safe. You may experience feelings of anxiety, anger, depressed hopelessness, and helplessness and disconnection. There will be ups and downs, optimism and despair. Take care of your spiritual needs to connect to your inner self. Your outward physical appearance is a small part of who you are. To use a prosthetic leg is like learning a new skill. The sky is the limit with a good prosthesis with a socket that fits...wear a sock over your stump. Wear the prosthetic leg when you get out of bed. Live your life and remove the leg at night.... A high stool in the kitchen is useful. Measure and set out all the ingredients on the bench before you cook. Use the back burner of the stove. The first public outing by yourself can very frightening."

So many things to learn. How to live with what I have done to my family? What will become of me? Will I always be remembered for trying to kill myself? I judge no one anymore. I am capable of everything.

Paula makes the pasties, positions them carefully on the baking tray, places them in the oven and sets the timer.

What evil genius made the pokies? Developed something that messed with people's minds, destroying them, hooking them. *For what? To make money out of people's misery?*

She holds a soapy sponge and wipes the bench with deep sweeps.

I have forgotten how to be happy.

I have been in crisis for years.

Addicted to avoidance.

EIGHTY-THREE

There is no cure for life
October 2010

PAULA, JENNY AND ADRIANNA ARE SEATED AROUND the wooden table at Paula's house. Scraps of leftover quiche, salad and empty wine glasses litter the table. It is 2 p.m., soft Braham's music wafts in the background. It is like old times. Lunch with friends. The alcohol has loosened voices which are getting louder.

"The bastard disappeared back to his wife," Jenny shouted.

"I hate all men."

"I never trusted him," Paula said in a measured tone.

Jenny glares at her.

"Who are you to judge?"

Paula adjusts her leg.

"My psychiatrist told me I have to tell the truth." She shrugs her shoulders. "It's not easy."

"Since you're telling the truth, perhaps you can tell us where you used to go when you were unavailable. Did you have a boyfriend?" asked Adrianna, her smooth face into Paula's.

"Hang on, Sam; that's harsh," said Jenny.

Paula is silent.

"At one stage. Briefly. I was seeing a stupid man. He made me laugh. But he broke my heart." Drops her voice.

"Colin doesn't know. I'm afraid to tell him. He's been so good since the train incident." She takes a breath. "Since I tried to kill myself." She blinks.

"But I intend to tell him. He deserves to know the truth about me." She swallows. "He may leave me. I would hate that."

"I knew there was something going on," said Adriana, her face smug and victorious.

"I always envied you, Adriana. A loving husband and luxurious home. Not having to work, unless you wanted to work. Children who never dabbled in drugs or ran with a bad crowd. You've been lucky."

Paula takes a drink of water. Holds the table to steady herself.

"Stop it," said Adriana, her voice irritated. "You see what you want to see." She reddens. "A year ago, I discovered my so called *loving husband* has a lover and there is child. My husband's child, a boy." She struggles to say the words.

"He...he...he bought her a flat and pays all her bills." She puts her hand to her throat. Her hands shake. "I don't know who I am anymore." She pours a glass of red wine. Sips it.

The others sit in silence waiting for her to continue.

"I am not a wife, but still married with all the financial perks of a marriage." Her face dares them not to say anything.

"We share a house and we *pretend* for our children." She gulps the rest of the wine in the glass. "He doesn't want a divorce. Neither do I." She breathes.

"What can I do? I haven't worked for years." In a small voice, adds, "And I enjoy our lifestyle, with the nice house and overseas trips and cruises." Adriana sniffs.

Paula reaches for a piece of cake. Jenny refills the glass for Adriana.

"All our lives are phony in some way. We all live a lie. I choose unattainable men as lovers. I'm the best judge of the worst men."

Jenny chuckles at her joke.

"Adriana lives the life we all want, but it's an illusion. Perfect Paula is not so perfect and tries to kill herself. Colin who's a cranky old bugger turns out to be a knight in shining armour." She gives a raucous laugh.

"A toast for us. We are illusionists. Still breathing, still friends."

They clink glasses.

"I want to share something with you," Paula spoke. "Tomorrow is my big adventure. I plan to go to the city by myself, using public transport. And not fall down on my face as I get off the tram."

"I'm determined to fly to England with Colin, visit Sarah and Buzz and my gorgeous little Simon. I want him to be proud of his grandma."

EIGHTY-FOUR

Nothing stays the same
November 2010

"RING ME WHEN YOU GET INTO TOWN OR HAVE ANY difficulties." His face looks worried.

She strokes his cheek.

"I need to do this myself."

Paula waits at the tram stop, holding the crutch for support. She climbs onto the tram as the therapist instructed. That part was achievable. Then the tram lurches forward sending her spinning in the aisle. She grabs the pole. The crutch clatters to the floor. She closes her eyes.

If I bend over to collect the crutch I'm going to lose my balance and fall.

A woman dressed in black picks the crutch and hands it to her.

"Thank you. I'm a bit shaky."

"Hang onto me. I'll help you."

There are no empty seats on the tram. Half a dozen students in uniform stare at their phones refusing to give up their seats. The woman glares at one student wearing a notable school uniform, sitting in the disabled seat, and talking on her phone. The student ignores her.

The woman in black takes out her mobile phone.

"I notice you are a student of St Columbus School. I might take your photo sitting while a disabled person stands. I am sure your headmaster would like to see it."

Four students jump from their seats.

"There's a seat," said the woman. "The kids just need a little lesson in manners."

"Thank you." Paula sits down. "I've had an amputation and I am not too good on my prosthesis yet."

"Where are you getting off?"

"St Paul's Cathedral."

"I'll make sure you don't fall down the steps." She stays close to Paula as she exits the tram. "You'll be fine now," said the woman.

"Thank you."

Paula examines the steps to the entrance to St Paul's Cathedral.

How on earth will I manage the steps?

She tries the first two steps but can't go any further. She sits on the nearby bench where a ragged man reeks of alcohol lies sprawled. He sits up when he sees her.

"Did you hurt your leg?" he asks.

She nods.

"Me and you are the same. I have a sore leg, too."

He rolls up his trousers and shows a scabby wound.

"Did you get hit by a car?" he asks, looking interested.

She hesitates. *Tell the truth.*

"I tried to kill myself. I didn't want to live, but I do now."

"I used pills. You get over it," he said. He passes Paula a brown paper bag.

"Do you want a sip?"

"Thanks for the offer but I need my wits about me to stay upright."

She walks to the pokies venue near the station. Watches the machines in their colour and sounds. Had planned to play the pokies for old time's sake. She watches hypnotized faces follow spinning reels.

I was one of those hypnotised people. It is over, the end of the love affair with the pokies.

She leaves the venue.

Her phone rings. "How are you doing?" asked Colin.

"Do you want me to pick you up?"

"I'll try to make it home," she said. "If you can meet me at the tram stop, that would be great."

"Text me when you are close."

I lost a leg, lost who I was, but I found something else. Me. And I am still alive.... I need to practice managing the underground in London…and deal with the hardest part of my life…face my daughter…tell her about my gambling…tell Colin about Rodney…. Will he ever forgive me?

The End

A Short List of Internet Support Services

Acquired brain injury

Information related to acquired brain injury treatment and counselling

International
> https://www.biausa.org/
> https://www.braintrauma.org/

Australia
Information related to acquired brain injury treatment and counselling
> https://www.braininjuryaustralia.org.au/
> http://www.arbias.org.au/
> http://www.brainlink.org.au/
> http://brainfoundation.org.au/disorders/
> acquired-brain-injury

Depression / suicide

Information related to depression and suicide treatment and counselling

International
> http://suicideprevention.wikia.com/wiki/USA

http://www.suicide.org/international-suicide-hotlines.html
http://www.suicidestop.com/call_a_hotline.html
https://www.iasp.info/resources/Crisis_Centres/

Australia
Information related to depression and suicide treatment and counselling
https://www.beyondblue.org.au/
https://www.lifeline.org.au/
https://kidshelpline.com.au/teens/issues/all-about-depression
https://www.healthdirect.gov.au/

Gambling

Information related to gambling treatment and counselling

International
https://www.ncpgambling.org/help-treatment/national-helpline-1-800-522-4700/

Gambling support groups and self help
https://www.gamblingtherapy.org/en/gamblers-anonymous-international-directory-world-wide-links

Australia
Information related to gambling treatment and counselling
https://www.gamblinghelponline.org.au/

https://gamblershelp.com.au/get-help/

Gambling support groups and self help
http://gaaustralia.org.au/members/

Substance abuse

Information related to substance abuse treatment
and counselling

International services

https://www.recovery.org/forums/
https://www.drugabuse.gov/publications/
principles-drug-addiction-treatment-research-
based-guide-third-edition/drug-addiction-
treatment-in-united-states

Substance abuse support groups and self help
http://www.navic.net.au/

Australia

Information related to substance abuse treatment
and counselling
Substance abuse treatment
http://www.directline.org.au/
https://www.counsellingonline.org.au/

Substance abuse support groups
http://www.navic.net.au/meetings/
http://www.fds.org.au/
http://www.sharc.org.au/family-drug-help/

www.ingramcontent.com/pod-product-compliance
Lightning Source LLC
Chambersburg PA
CBHW030341120726
47901CB00007B/1869